FAR OUT
CLASSIC STORIES

STONE ARCH BOOKS
a capstone imprint

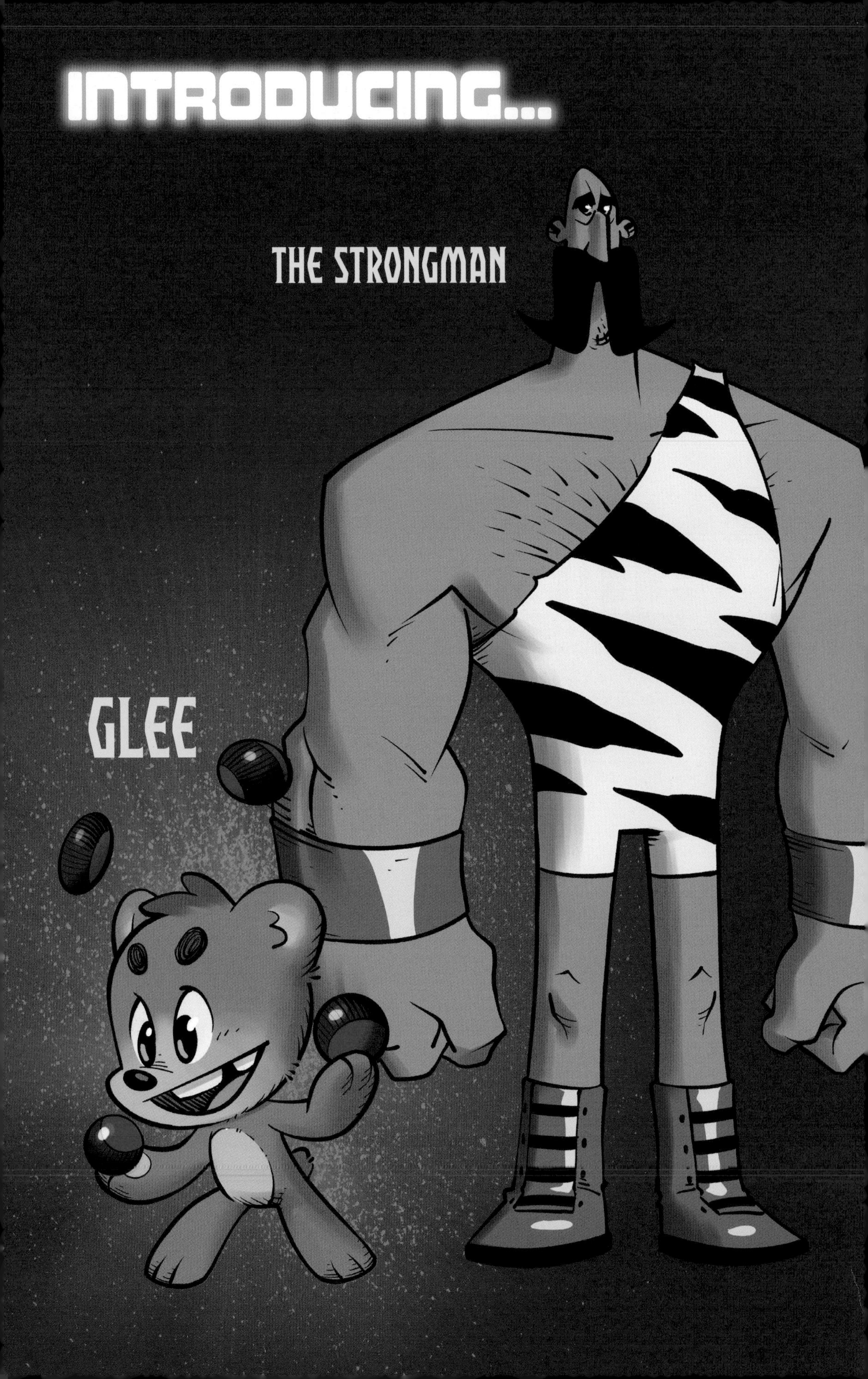
INTRODUCING...
THE STRONGMAN
GLEE

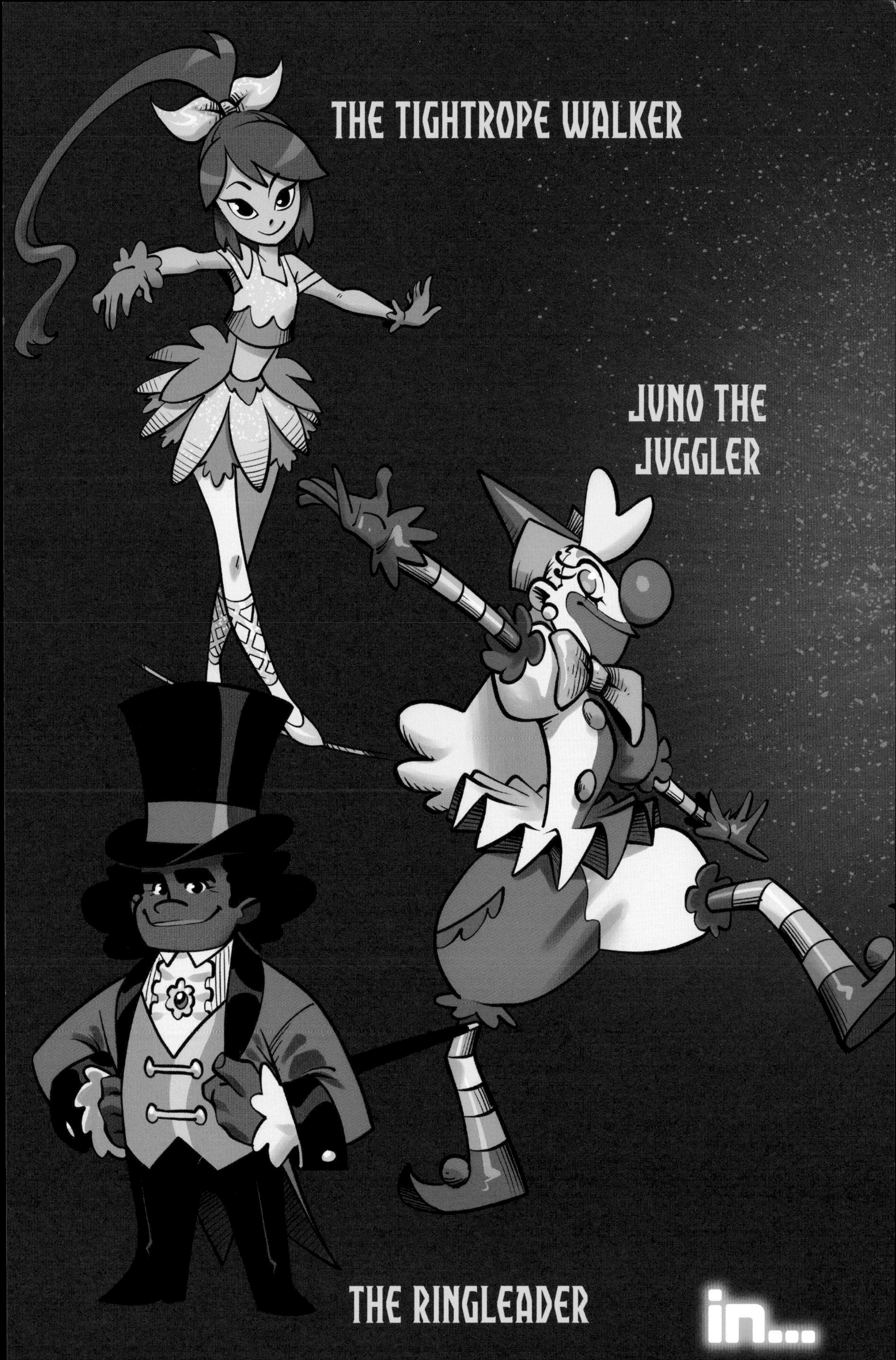
THE TIGHTROPE WALKER
JUNO THE JUGGLER
THE RINGLEADER
in...

Published by Stone Arch Books,
an imprint of Capstone.
1710 Roe Crest Drive
North Mankato, Minnesota 56003
capstonepub.com

Library of Congress Cataloging-in-Publication Data
Names: Peters, Stephanie True, 1965- author. I Lozano, Omar, illustrator.
Title: The juggle book : a graphic novel / by Stephanie True Peters ; illustrated by Omar Lozano.
Description: North Mankato, Minnesota : Stone Arch Books, an imprint of Capstone, [2022] I Series: Far out classic stories I Audience: Ages 8-11. I Audience: Grades 4-6. I Summary: In this graphic novel loosely based on Rudyard Kipling's "The Jungle Book," an orphaned bear cub named Glee finds a new home in a traveling circus.
Identifiers: LCCN 2021029882 (print) I LCCN 2021029883 (ebook) I ISBN 9781663977090 (hardcover) I ISBN 9781666330205 (paperback) I ISBN 9781666330212 (pdf) I ISBN 9781666330236 (kindle edition)
Subjects: LCSH: Bear cubs—Comic books, strips, etc. I Bear cubs—Juvenile fiction. I Circus performers—Comic books, strips, etc. I Circus performers—Juvenile fiction. I Juggling—Comic books, strips, etc. I Juggling—Juvenile fiction. I Graphic novels. I CYAC: Graphic novels. I Bears—Fiction. I Circus—Fiction. I Ability—Fiction. I Juggling—Fiction. I LCGFT: Graphic novels.
Classification: LCC PZ7.7.P44 Ju 2022 (print) I LCC PZ7.7.P44 (ebook) I DDC 741.5/973—dc23
LC record available at https://lccn.loc.gov/2021029882
LC ebook record available at https://lccn.loc.gov/2021029883

Designed by Hilary Wacholz
Edited by Mandy Robbins
Lettered by Jaymes Reed

Printed and bound in the USA. PO4608

FAR OUT CLASSIC STORIES

THE JUGGLE BOOK

A GRAPHIC NOVEL

BY STEPHANIE TRUE PETERS

ILLUSTRATED BY OMAR LOZANO

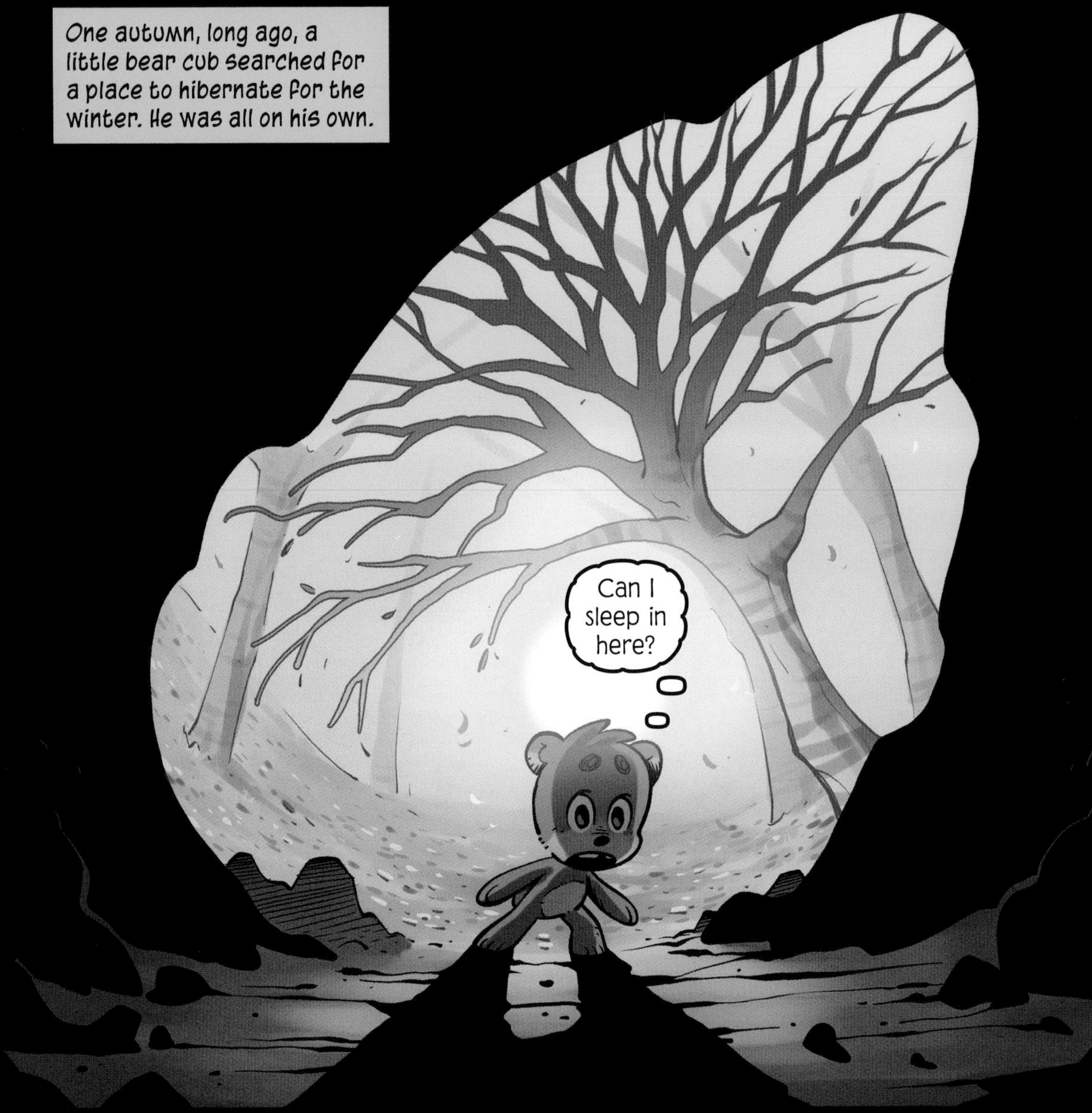
One autumn, long ago, a little bear cub searched for a place to hibernate for the winter. He was all on his own.
Can I sleep in here?

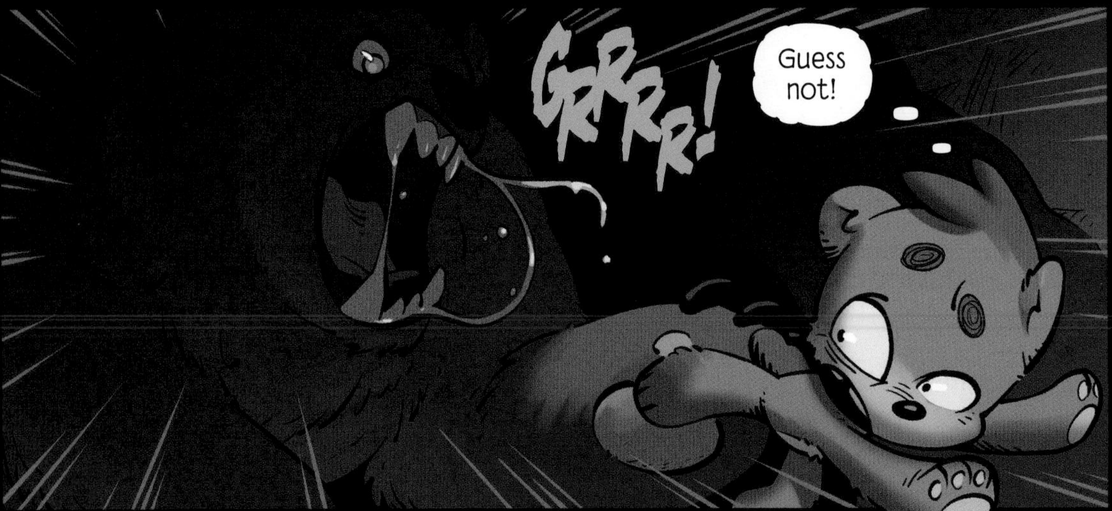
GRRRR!
Guess not!

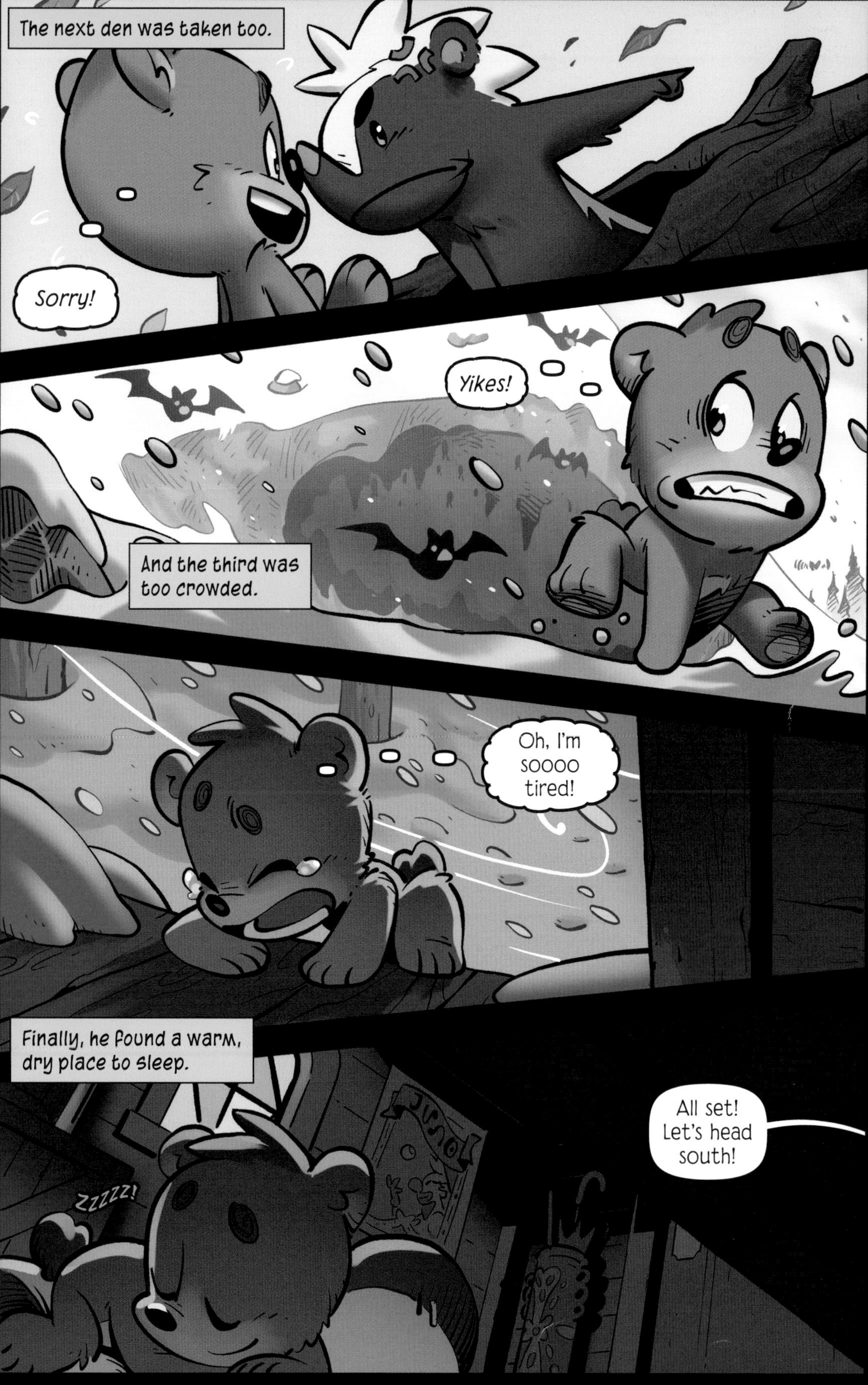
The next den was taken too.
Sorry!
Yikes!
And the third was too crowded.
Oh, I'm soooo tired!
Finally, he found a warm, dry place to sleep.
All set! Let's head south!
ZZZZZ!

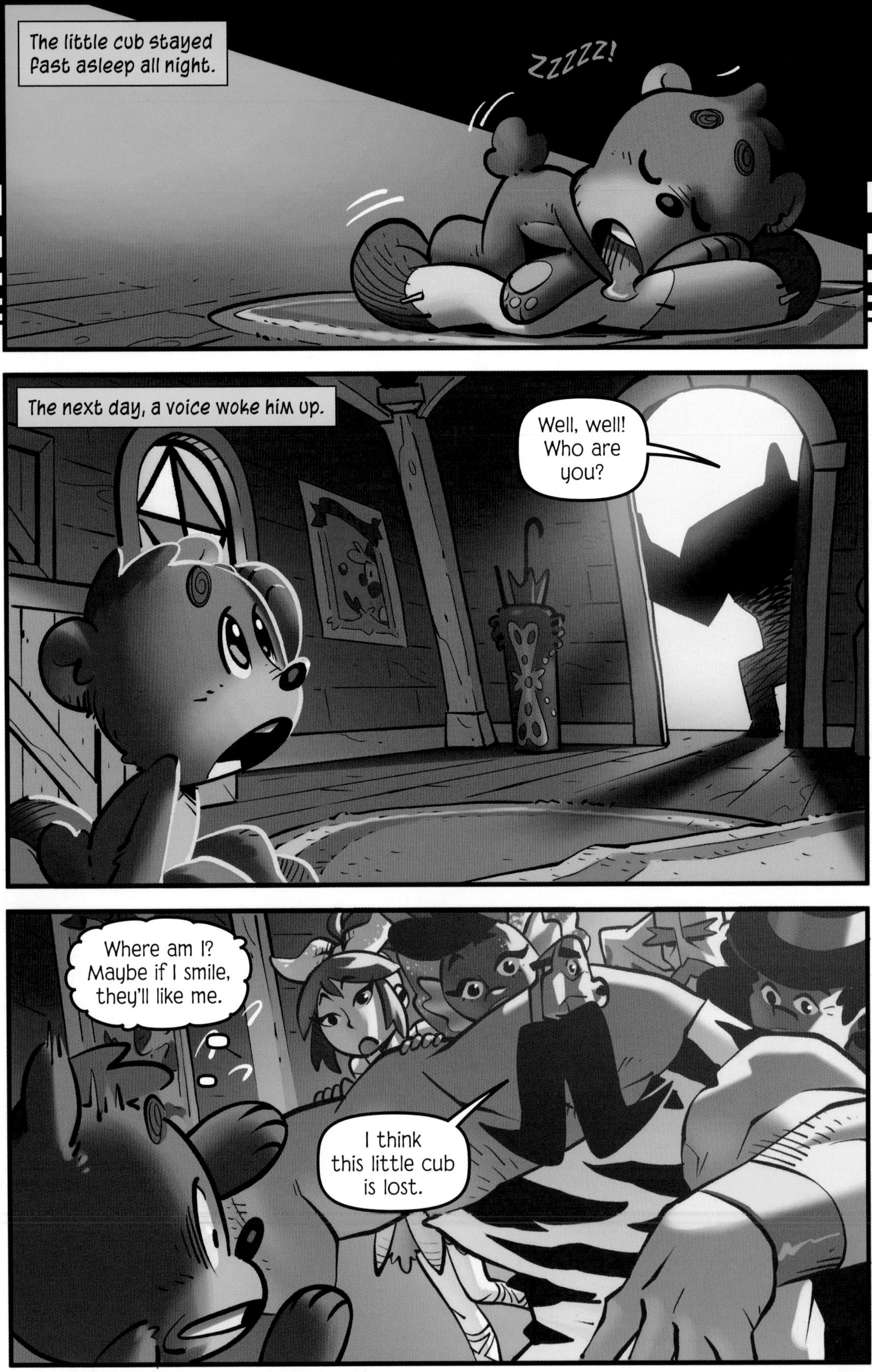
The little cub stayed fast asleep all night.
ZZZZZ!
The next day, a voice woke him up.
Well, well! Who are you?
Where am I? Maybe if I smile, they'll like me.
I think this little cub is lost.

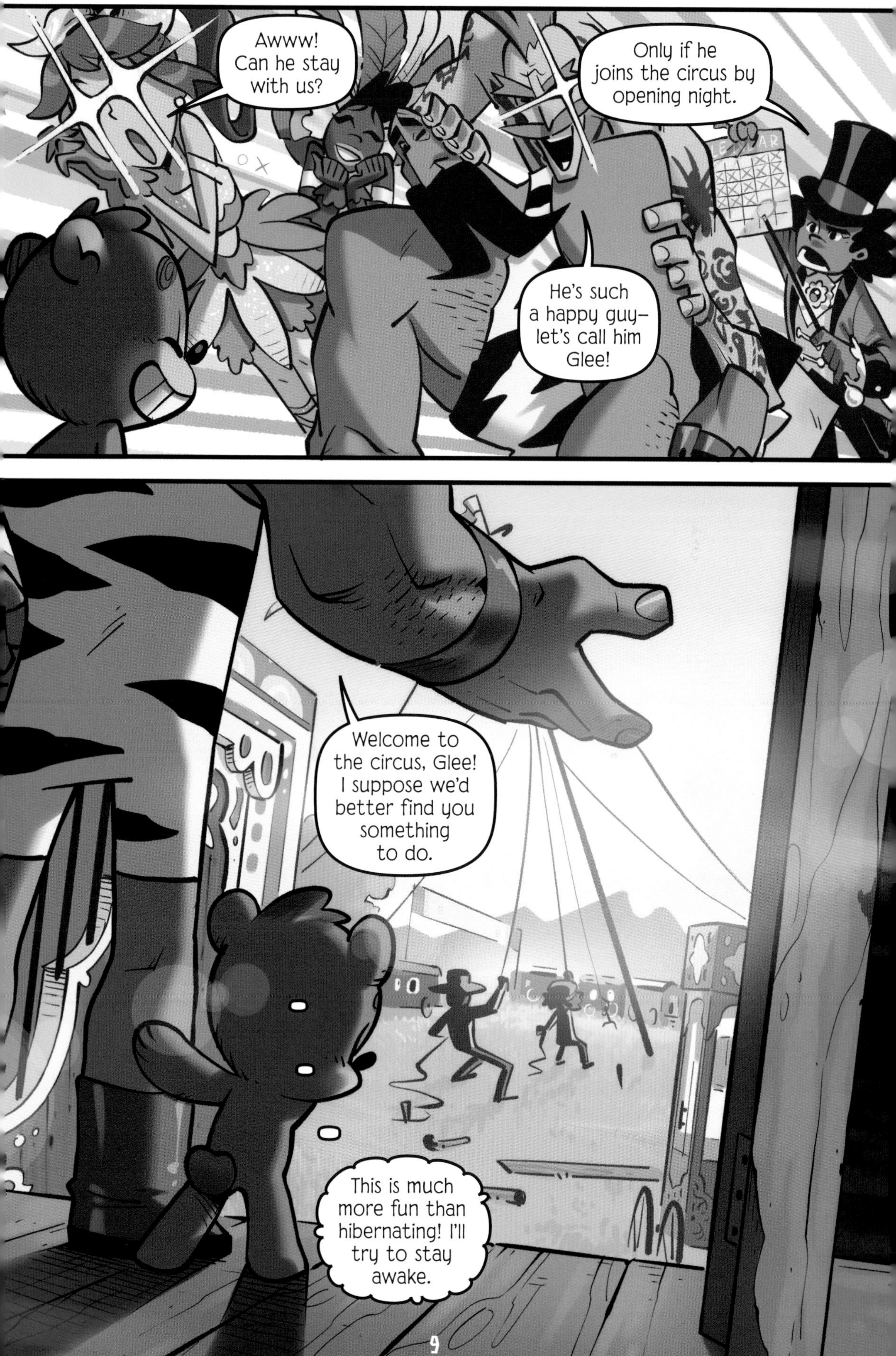
Awww! Can he stay with us?
Only if he joins the circus by opening night.
He's such a happy guy—let's call him Glee!
Welcome to the circus, Glee! I suppose we'd better find you something to do.
This is much more fun than hibernating! I'll try to stay awake.

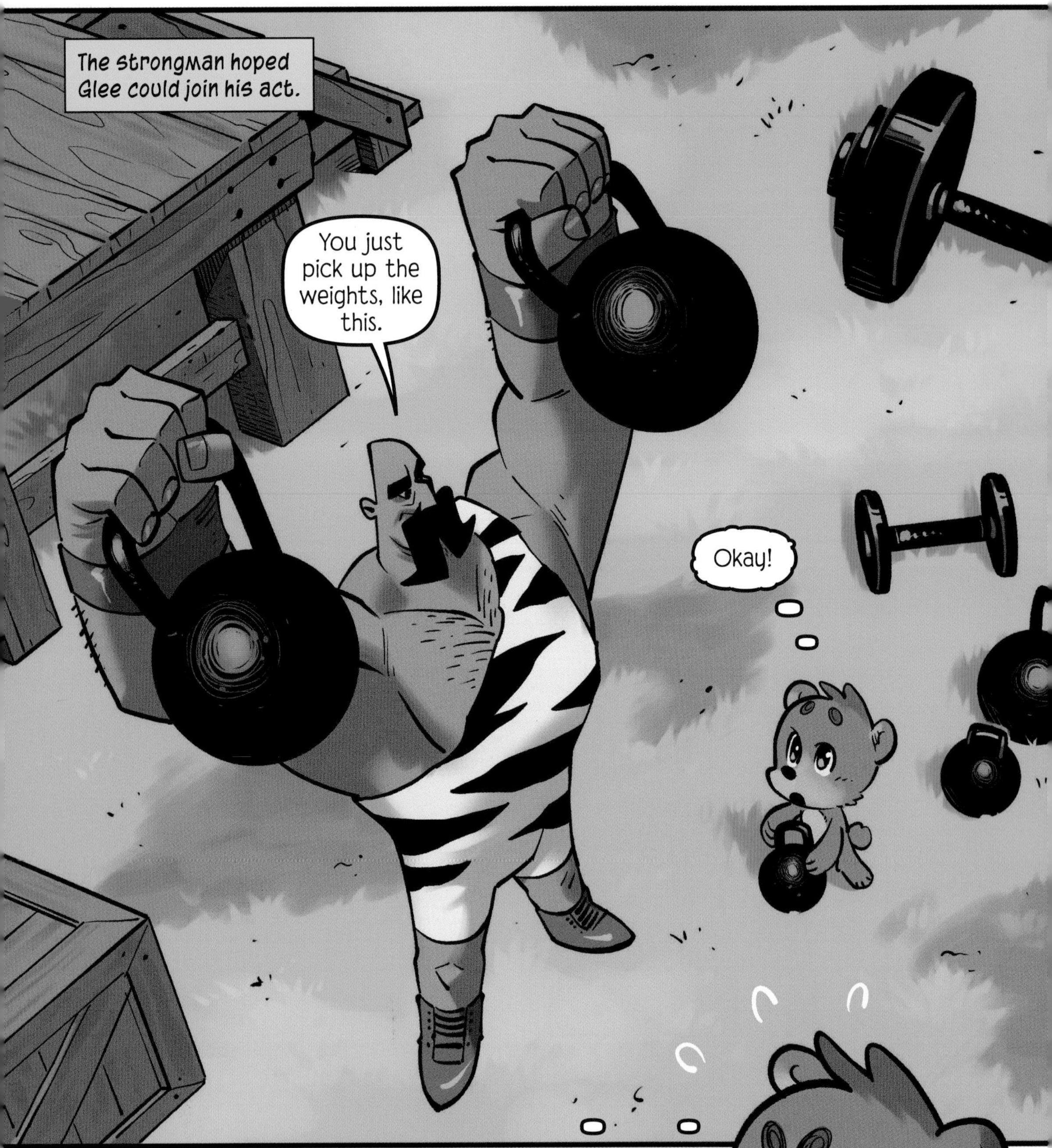

The strongman hoped Glee could join his act.
You just pick up the weights, like this.
Okay!

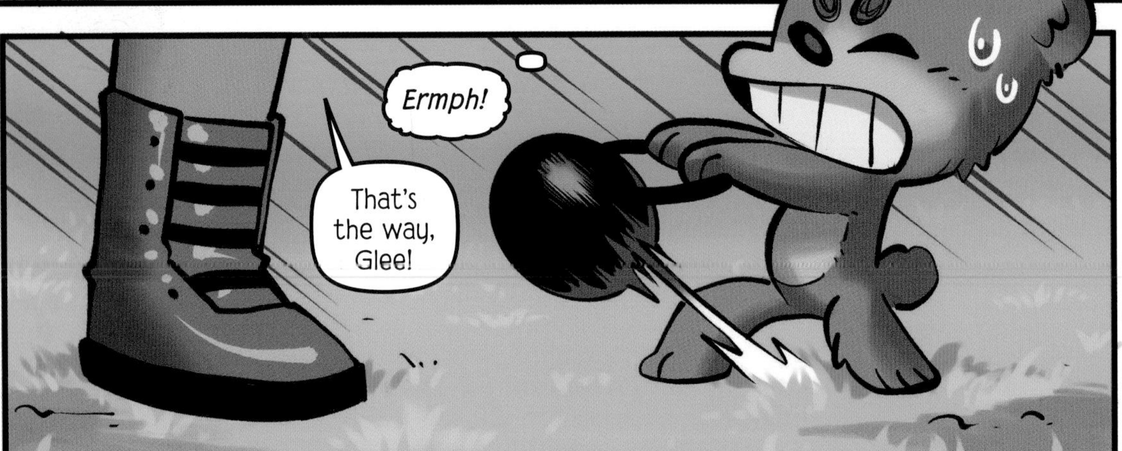

Ermph!
That's the way, Glee!

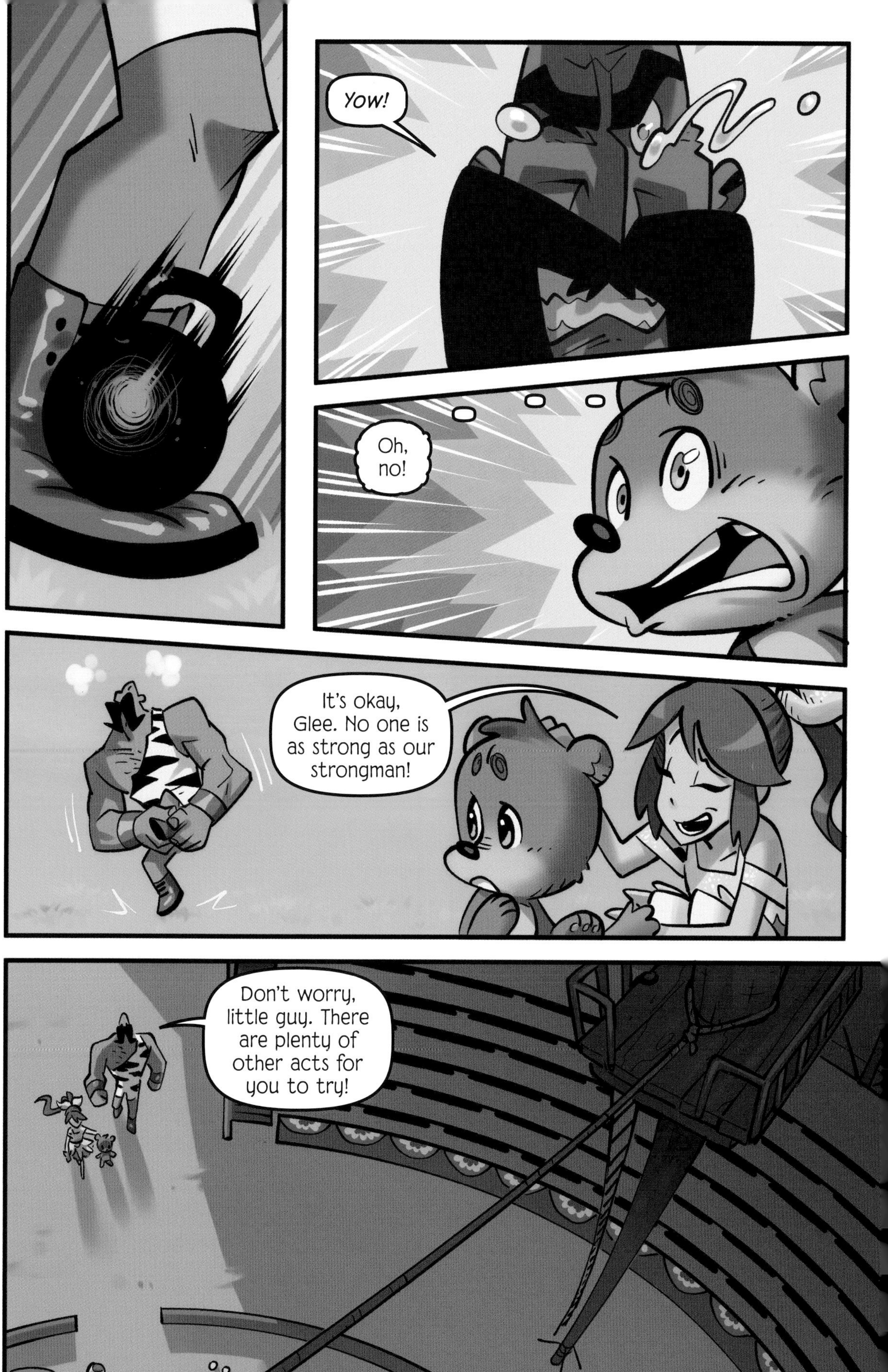
YOW!
Oh, no!
It's okay, Glee. No one is as strong as our strongman!
Don't worry, little guy. There are plenty of other acts for you to try!

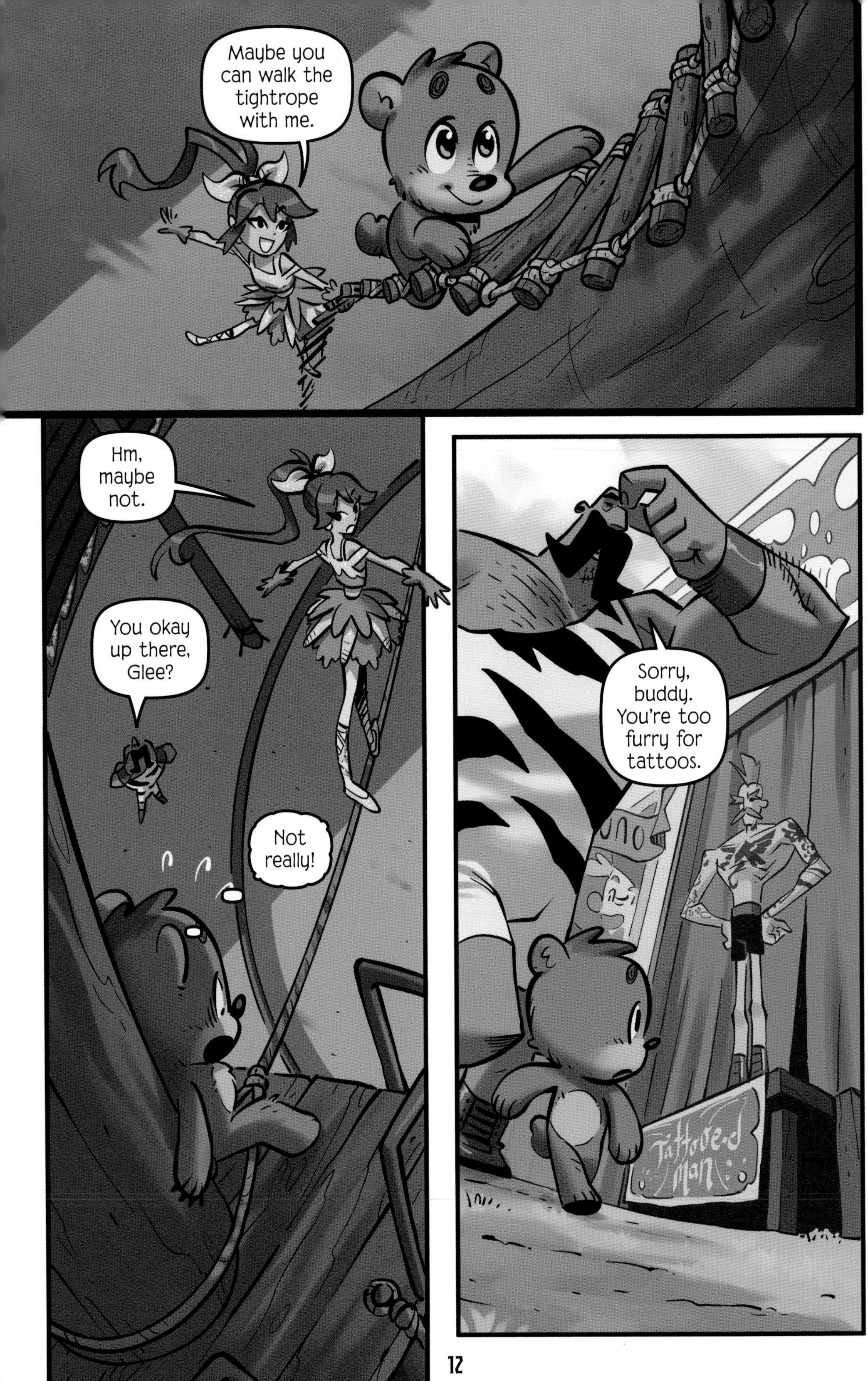
Maybe you can walk the tightrope with me.
Hm, maybe not.
You okay up there, Glee?
Not really!
Sorry, buddy. You're too furry for tattoos.
Tattooed Man

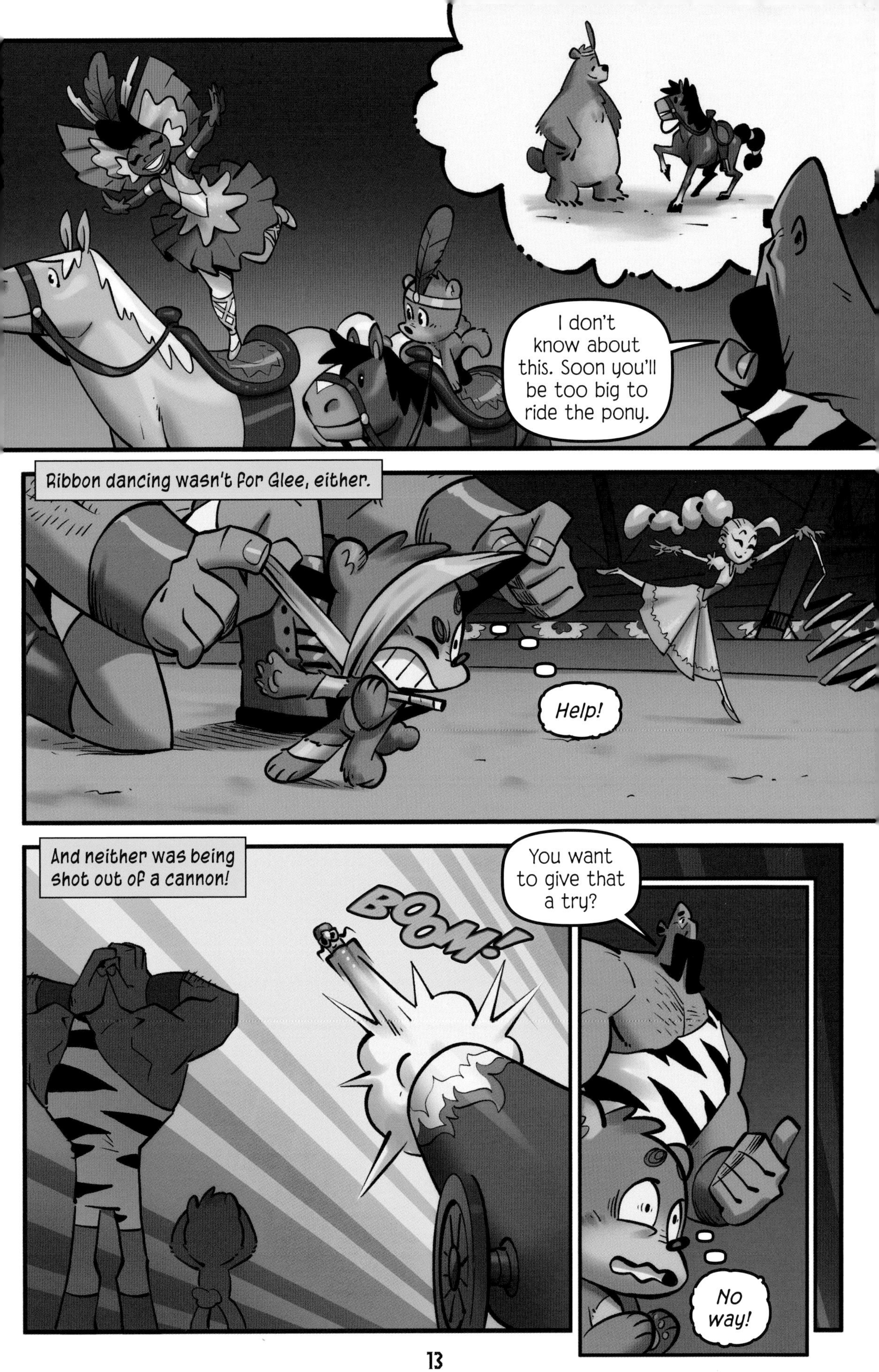
I don't know about this. Soon you'll be too big to ride the pony.
Ribbon dancing wasn't for Glee, either.
Help!
And neither was being shot out of a cannon!
BOOM!
You want to give that a try?
No way!

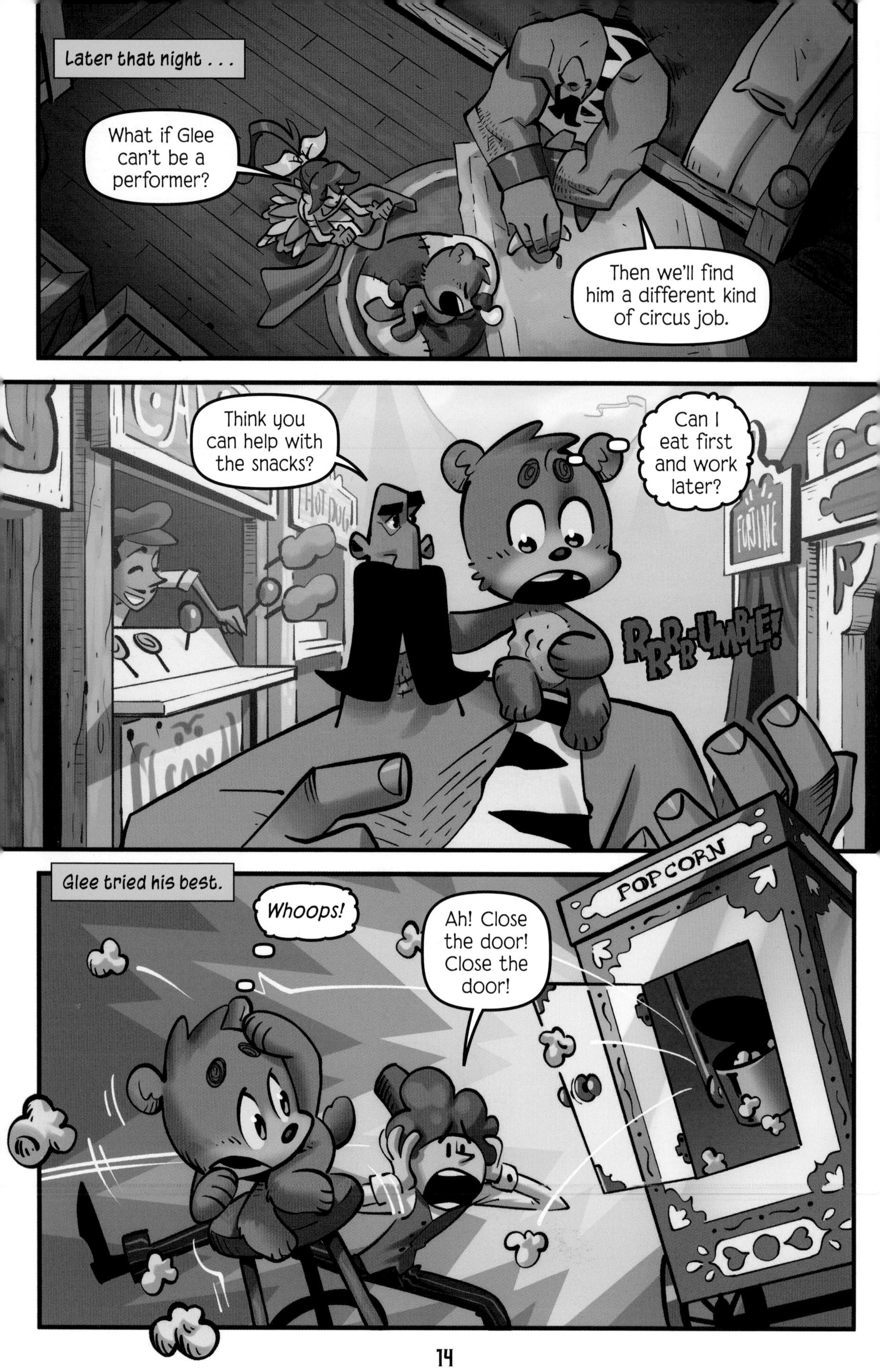
Later that night . . .
What if Glee can't be a performer?
Then we'll find him a different kind of circus job.
Think you can help with the snacks?
Can I eat first and work later?
HOT DOG
FORTUNE
RRRR-UMBLE!
Glee tried his best.
Whoops!
Ah! Close the door! Close the door!
POPCORN

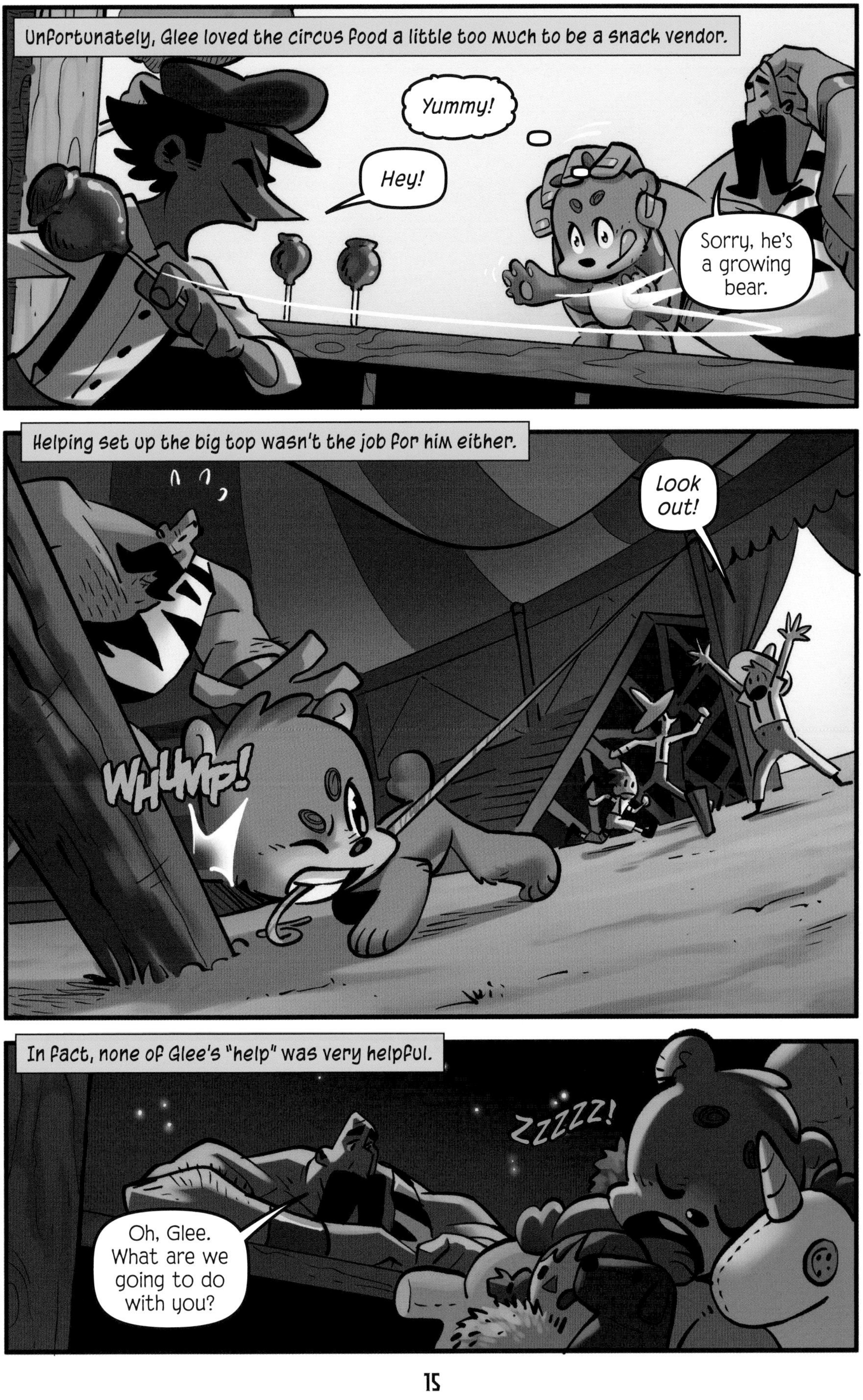

Unfortunately, Glee loved the circus food a little too much to be a snack vendor.
Yummy!
Hey!
Sorry, he's a growing bear.
Helping set up the big top wasn't the job for him either.
Look out!
WHUMP!
In fact, none of Glee's "help" was very helpful.
ZZZZZ!
Oh, Glee. What are we going to do with you?

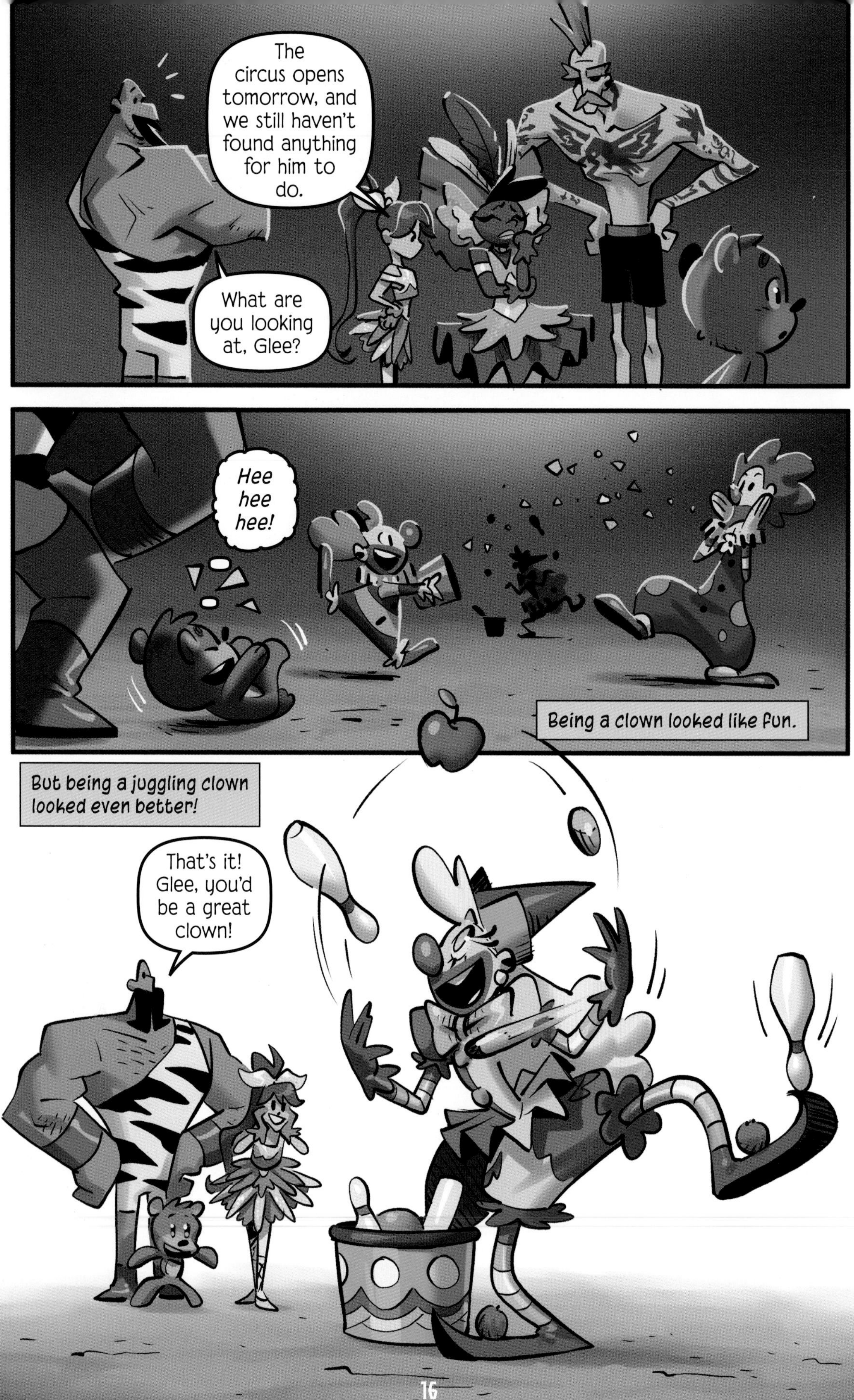

The circus opens tomorrow, and we still haven't found anything for him to do.
What are you looking at, Glee?
Hee hee hee!
Being a clown looked like fun.
But being a juggling clown looked even better!
That's it! Glee, you'd be a great clown!

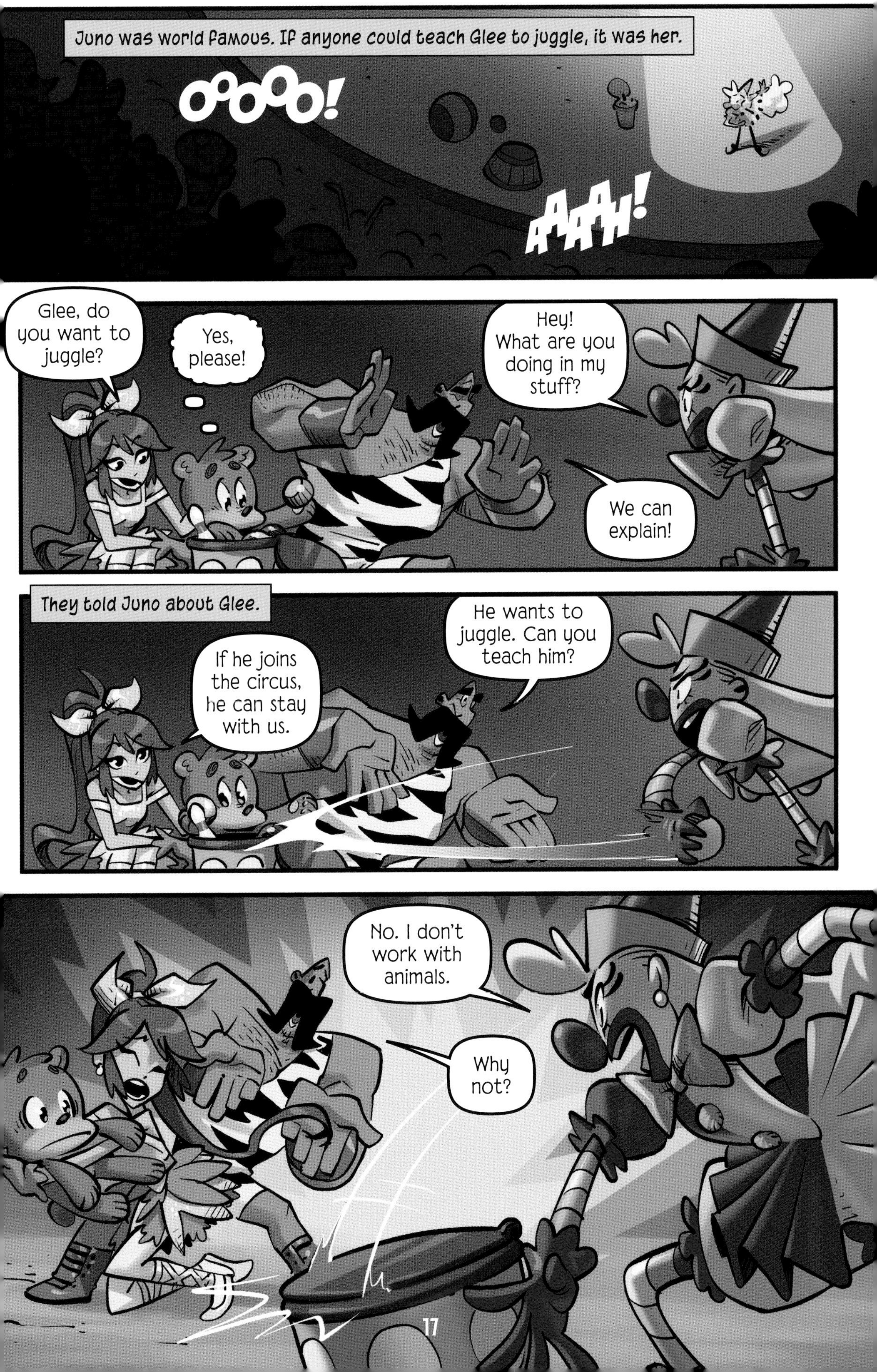
Juno was world famous. If anyone could teach Glee to juggle, it was her.
OoOoO!
AAAAH!
Glee, do you want to juggle?
Yes, please!
Hey! What are you doing in my stuff?
We can explain!
They told Juno about Glee.
He wants to juggle. Can you teach him?
If he joins the circus, he can stay with us.
No. I don't work with animals.
Why not?

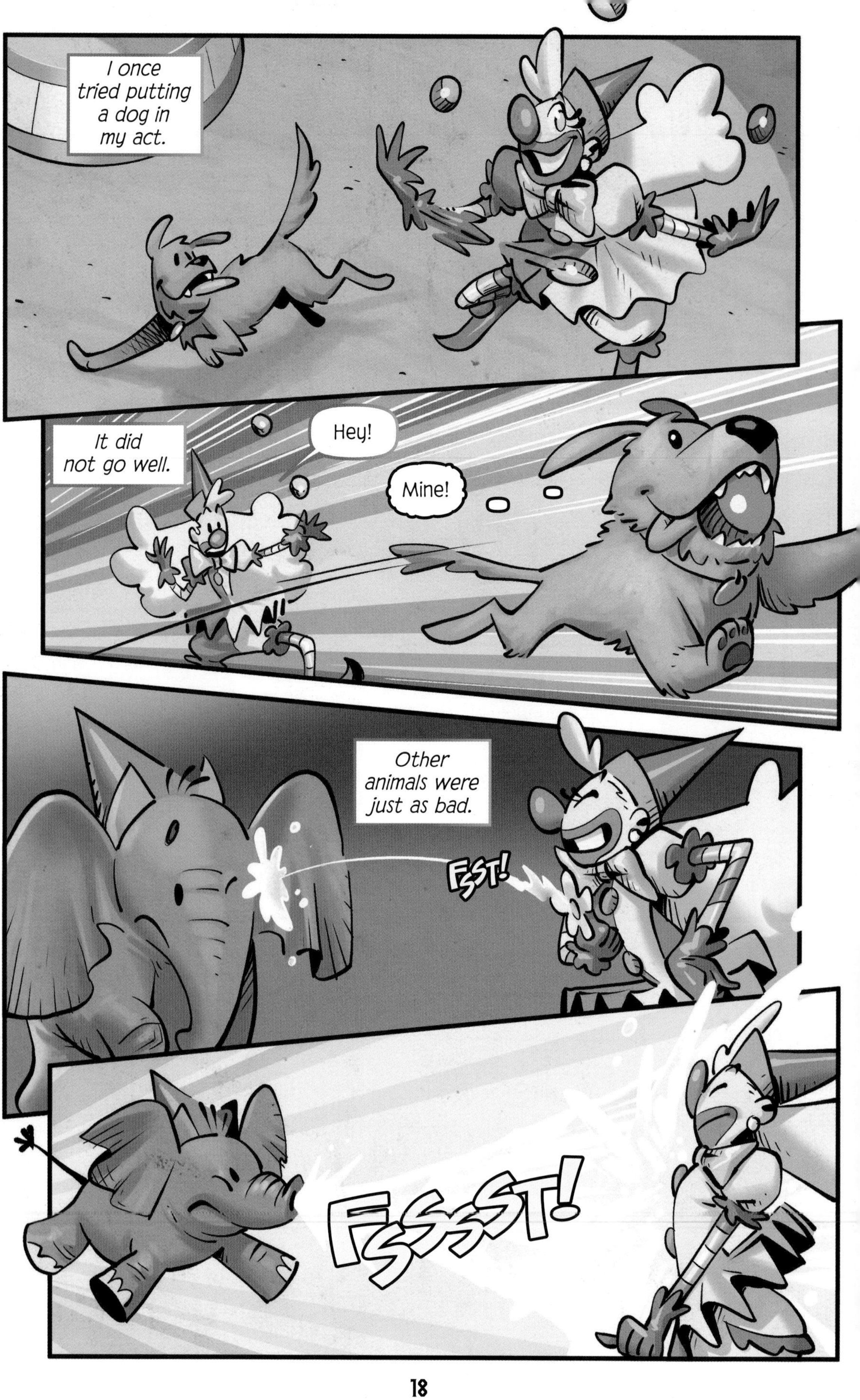
I once tried putting a dog in my act.
It did not go well.
Hey!
Mine!
Other animals were just as bad.
FSST!
FSSSST!

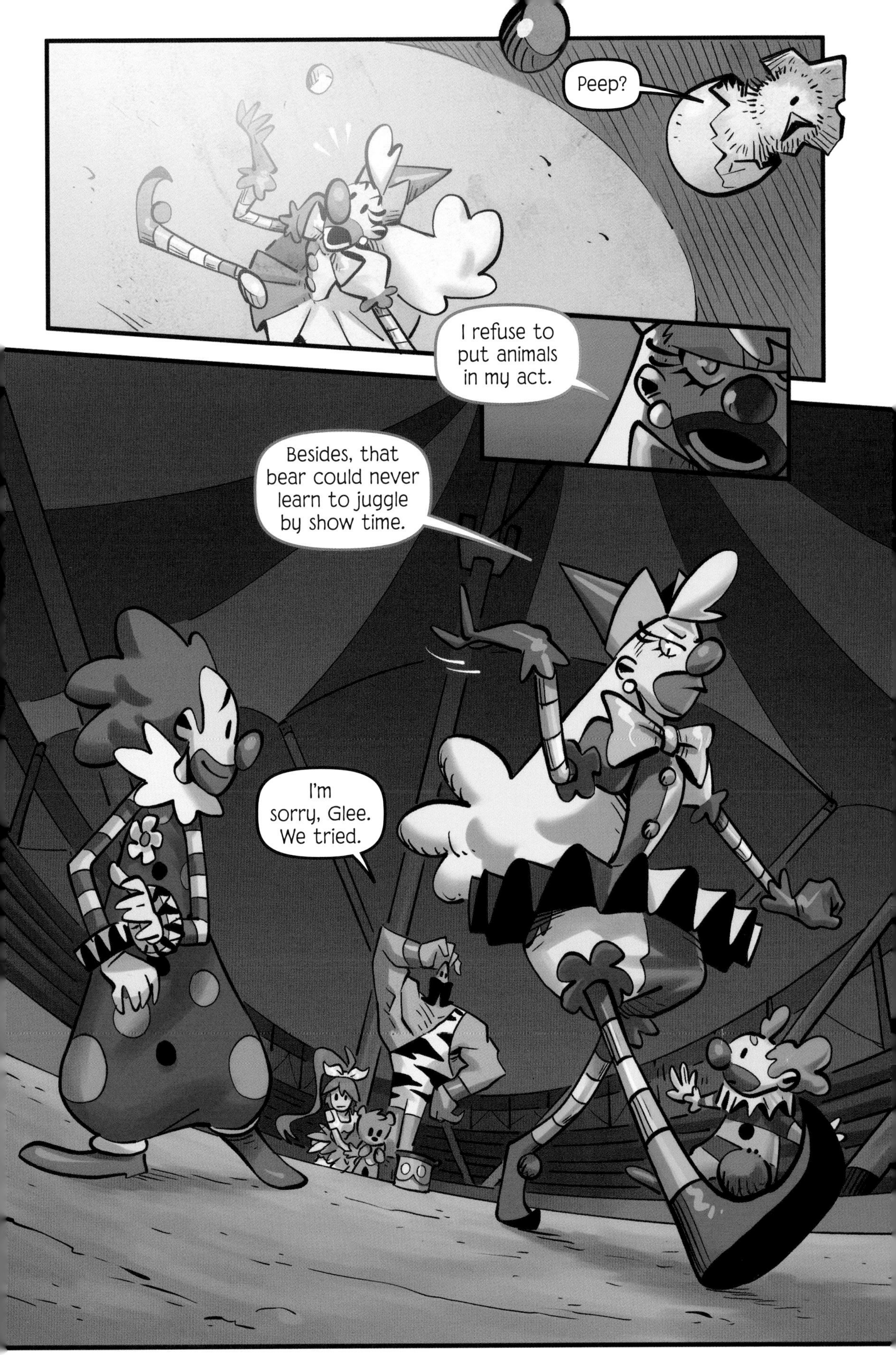
Peep?
I refuse to put animals in my act.
Besides, that bear could never learn to juggle by show time.
I'm sorry, Glee. We tried.

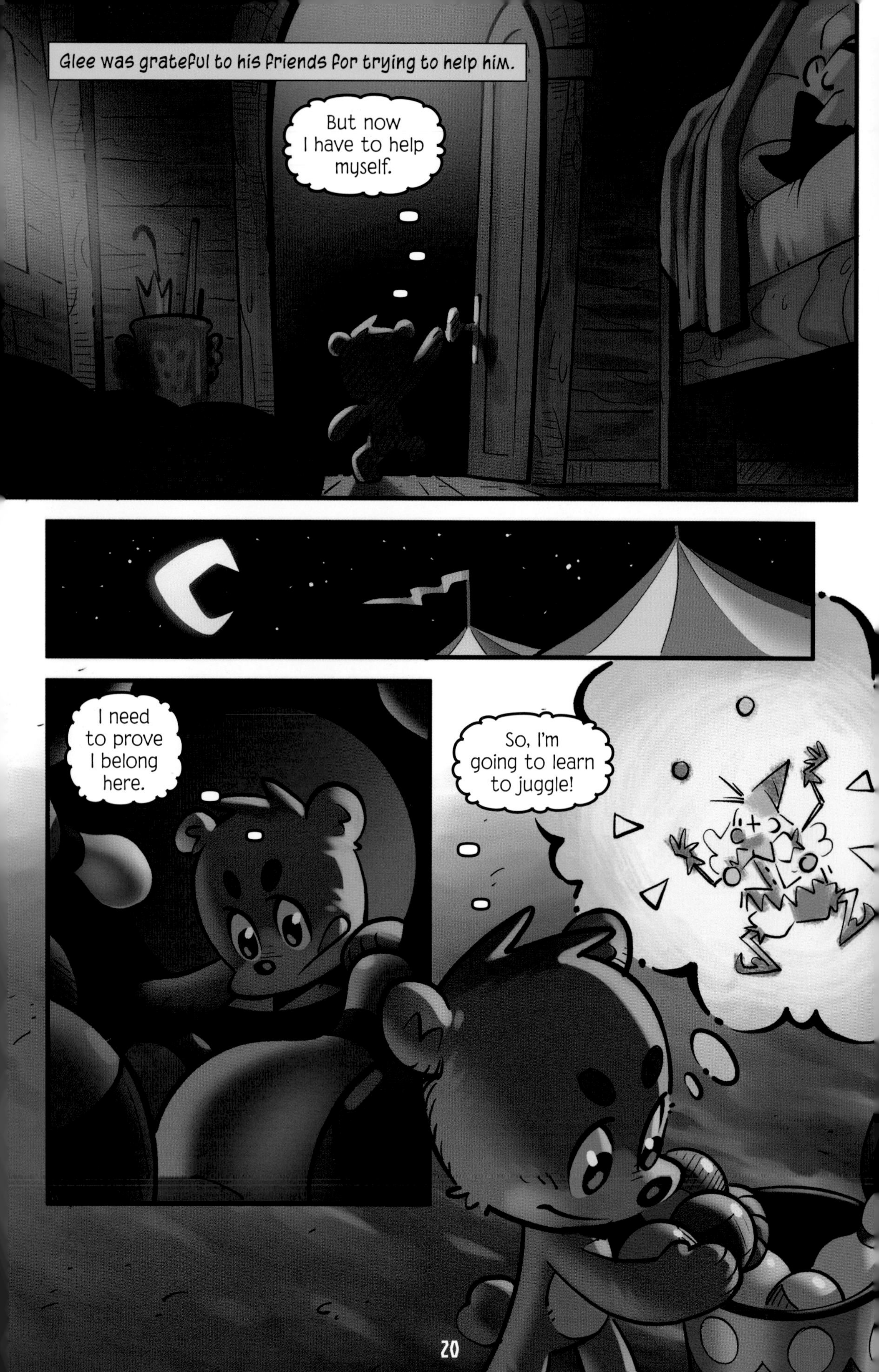
Glee was grateful to his friends for trying to help him.
But now I have to help myself.
I need to prove I belong here.
So, I'm going to learn to juggle!

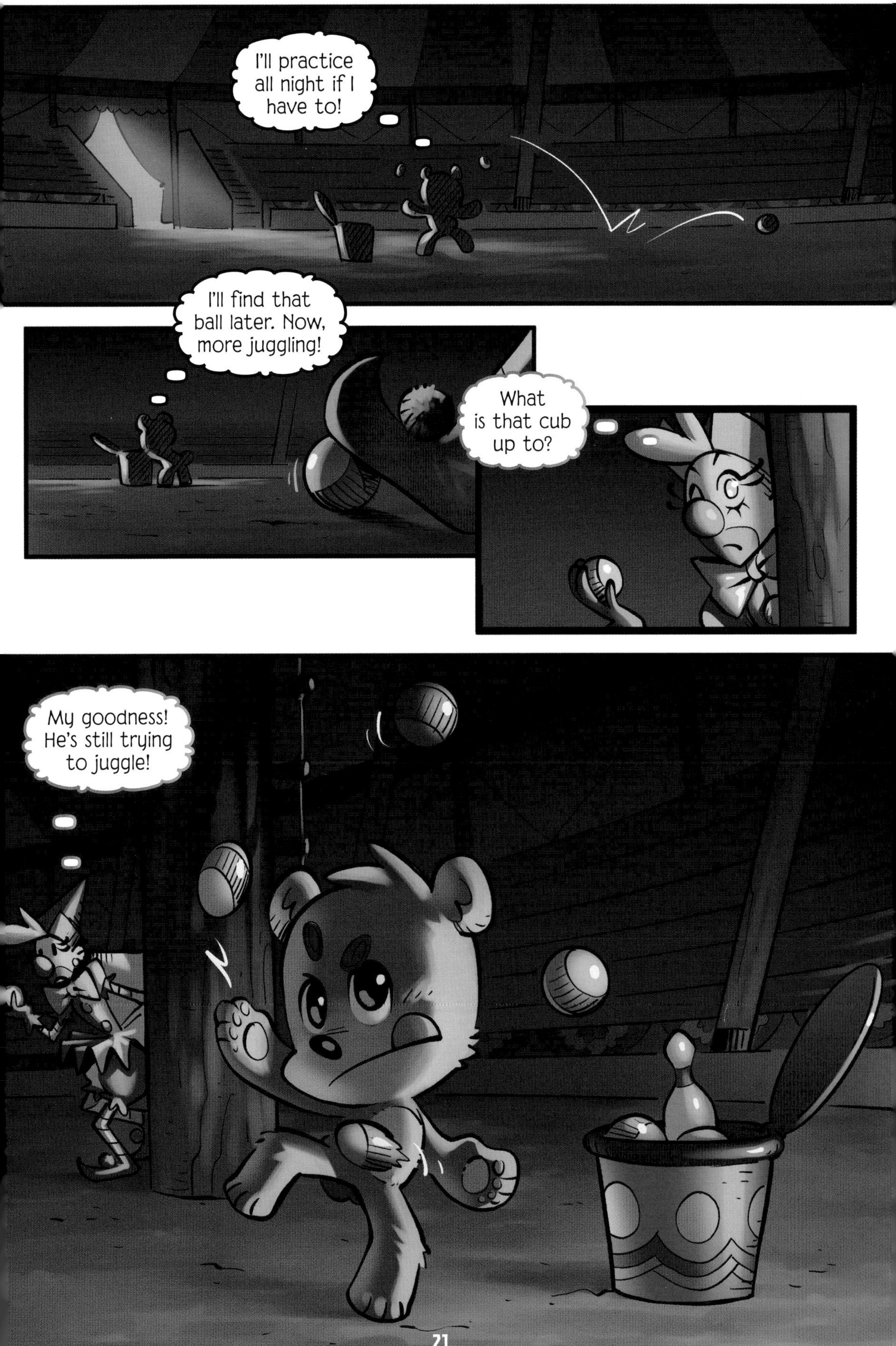
I'll practice all night if I have to!
I'll find that ball later. Now, more juggling!
What is that cub up to?
My goodness! He's still trying to juggle!

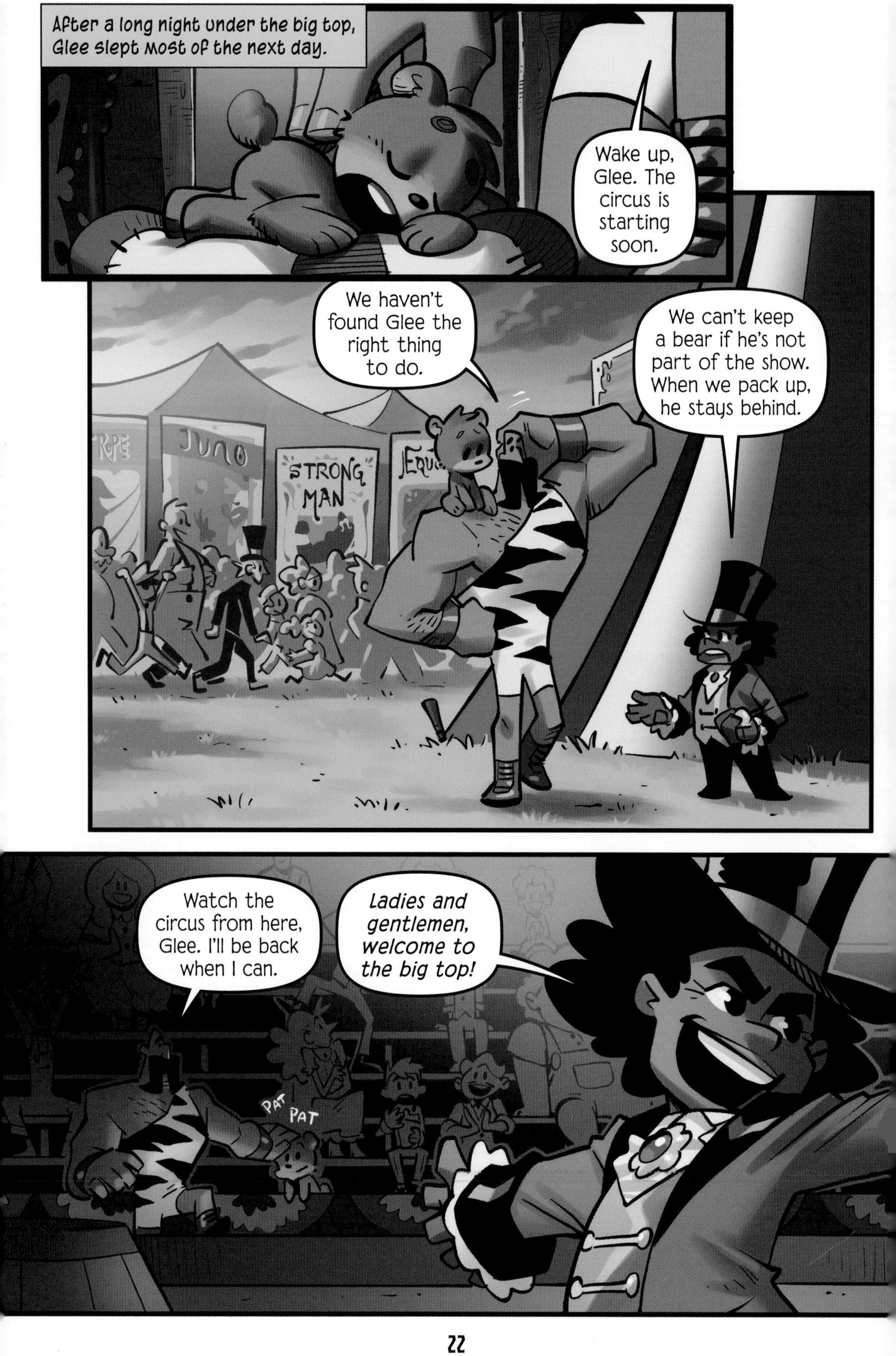
After a long night under the big top, Glee slept most of the next day.
Wake up, Glee. The circus is starting soon.
We haven't found Glee the right thing to do.
We can't keep a bear if he's not part of the show. When we pack up, he stays behind.
JUNO
STRONG MAN
Watch the circus from here, Glee. I'll be back when I can.
Ladies and gentlemen, welcome to the big top!
PAT PAT

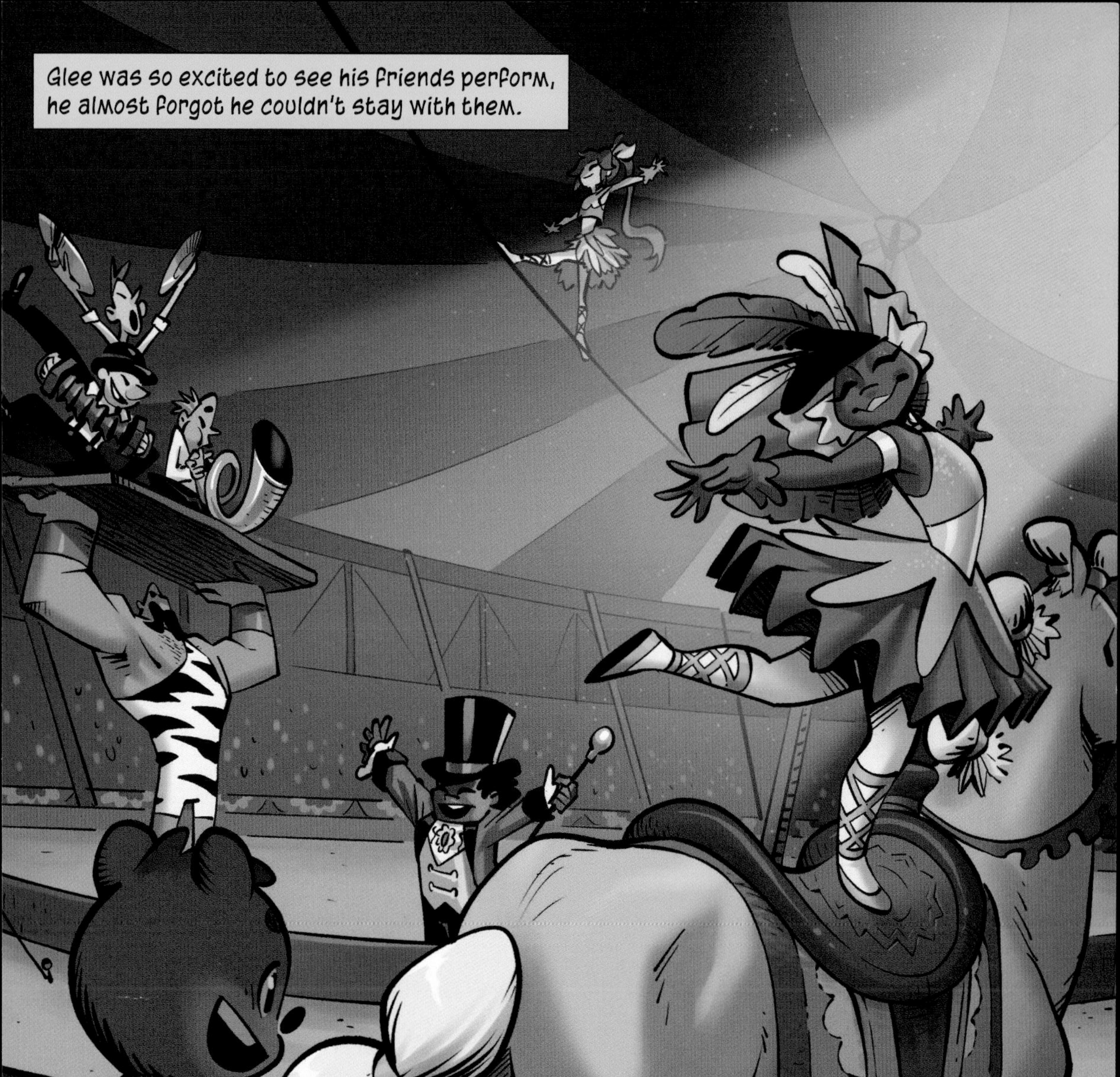
Glee was so excited to see his friends perform, he almost forgot he couldn't stay with them.

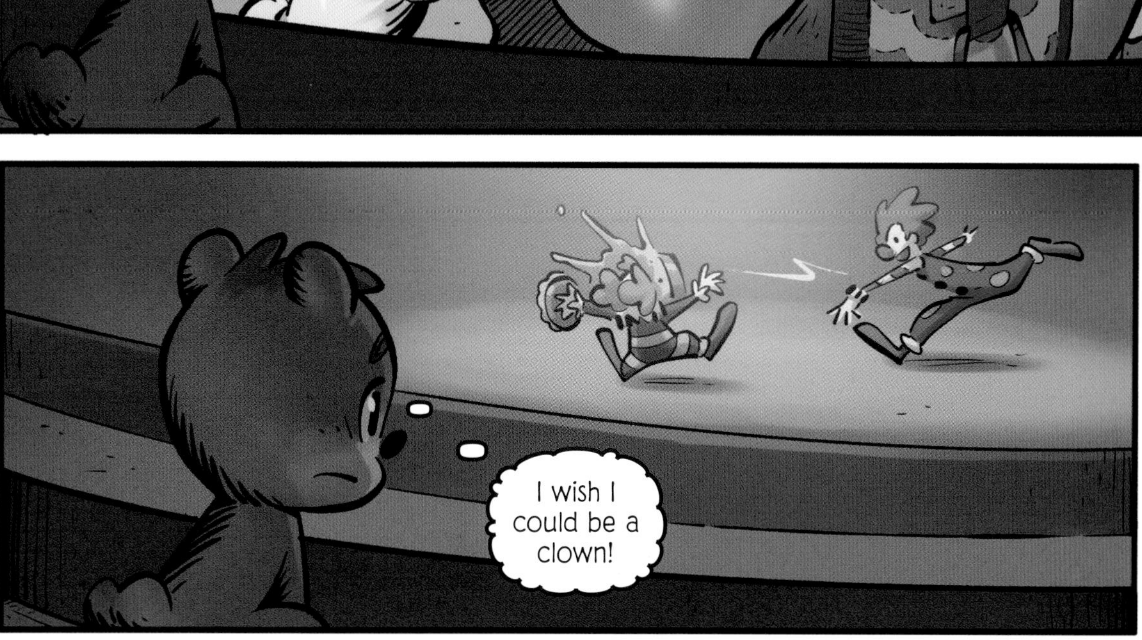
I wish I could be a clown!

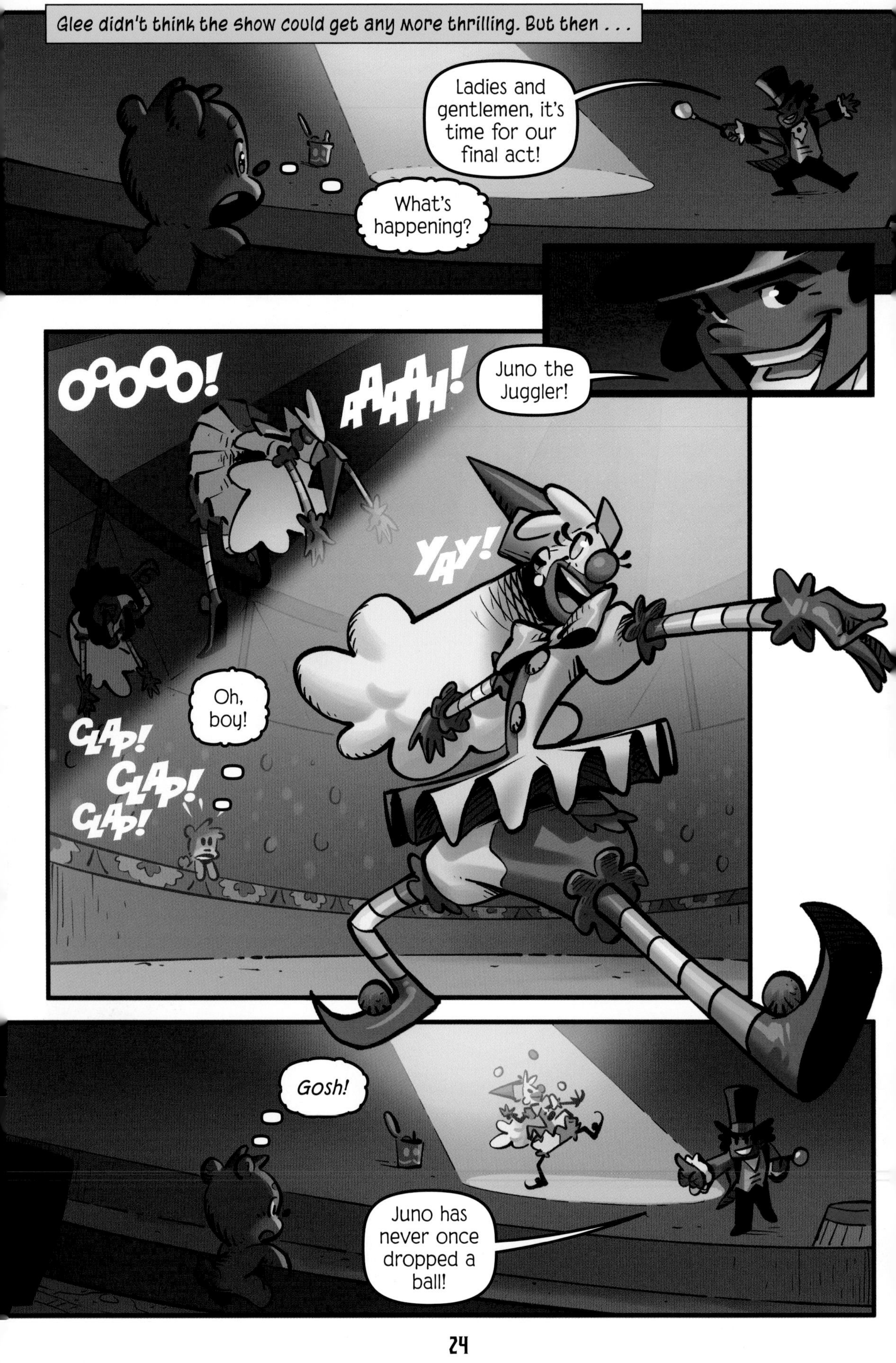

Glee didn't think the show could get any more thrilling. But then . . .
Ladies and gentlemen, it's time for our final act!
What's happening?
Juno the Juggler!
OOOOO!
AAAAH!
YAY!
Oh, boy!
CLAP!
CLAP!
CLAP!
Gosh!
Juno has never once dropped a ball!

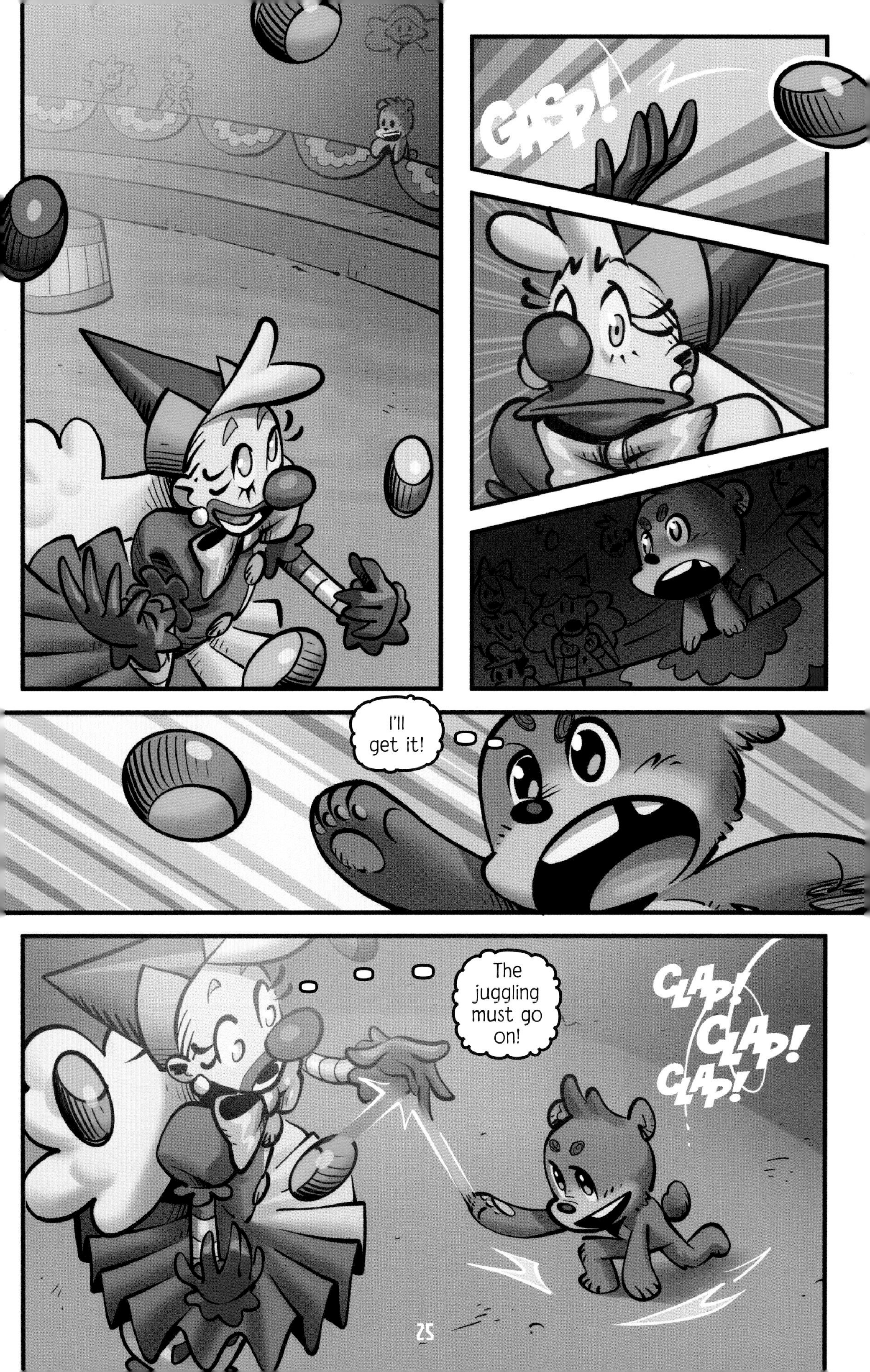
GASP!
I'll get it!
The juggling must go on!
CLAP! CLAP! CLAP!

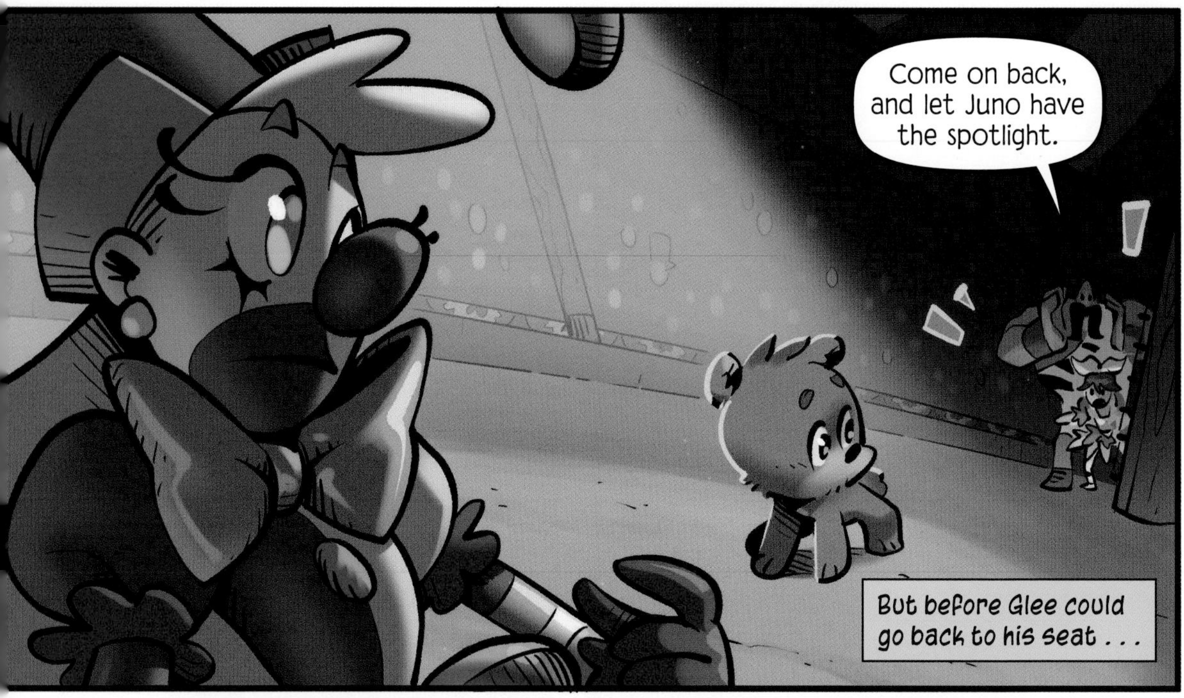
Come on back, and let Juno have the spotlight.
But before Glee could go back to his seat . . .

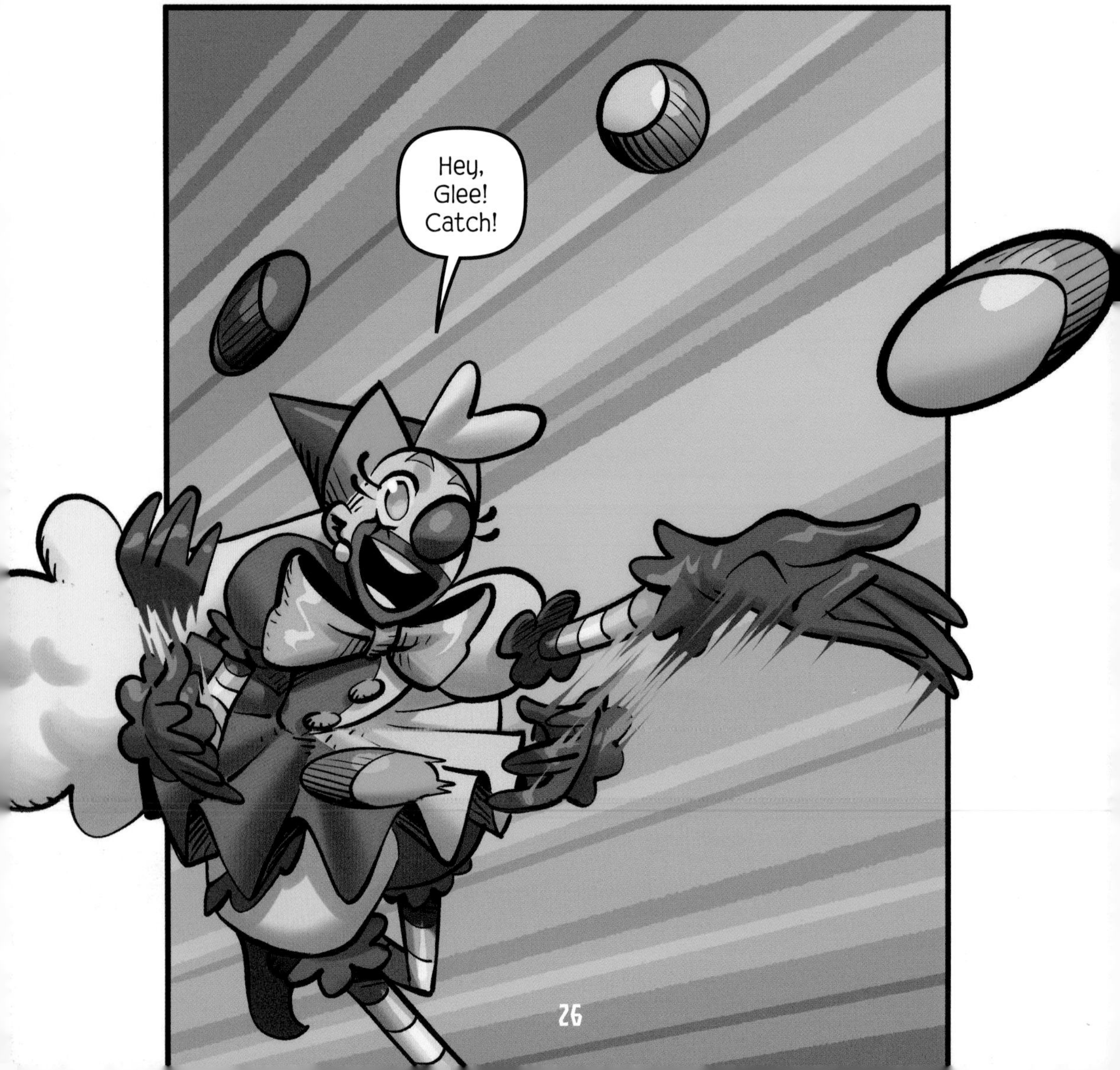
Hey, Glee! Catch!

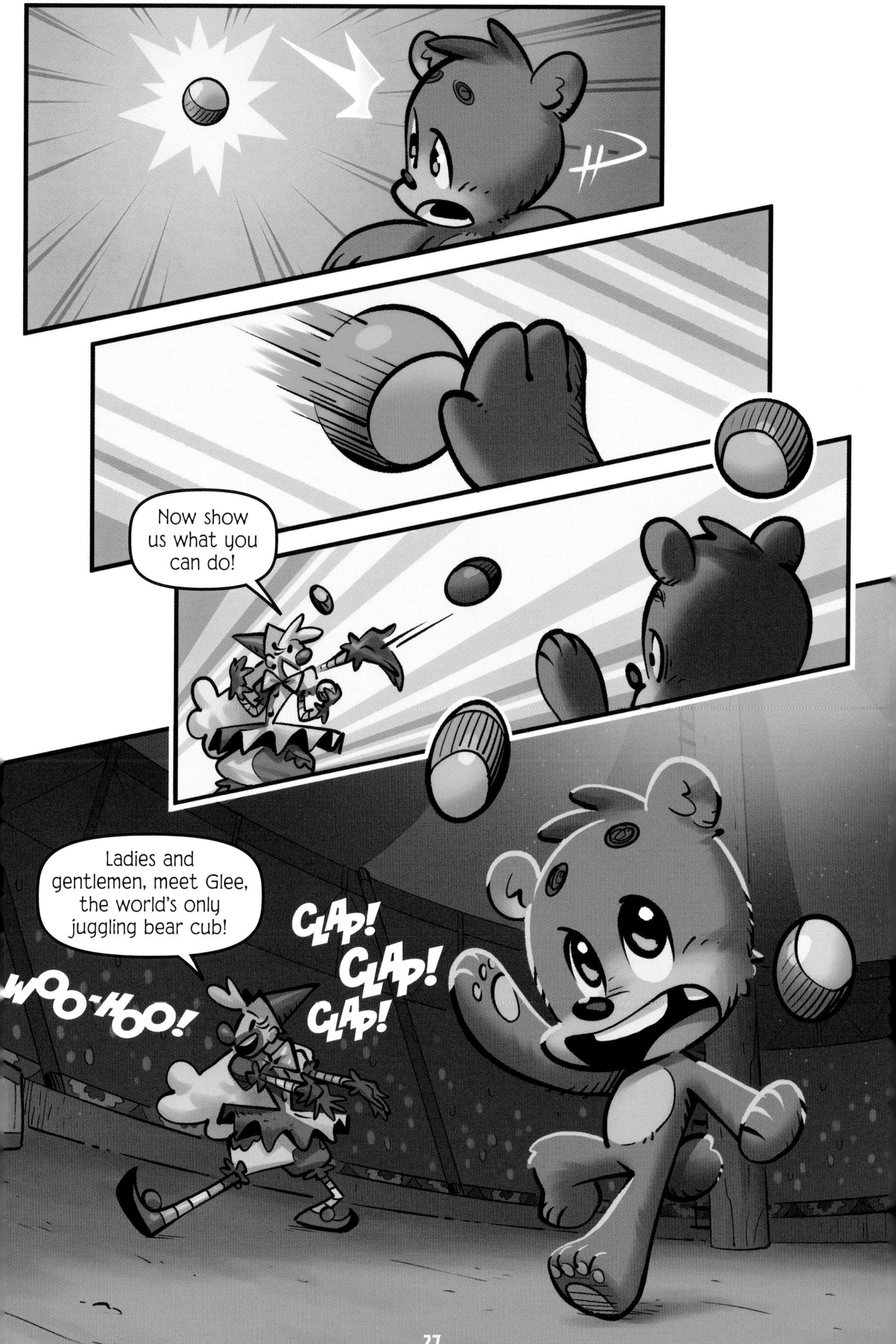
Now show us what you can do!
Ladies and gentlemen, meet Glee, the world's only juggling bear cub!
CLAP!
CLAP!
CLAP!
WOO-HOO!

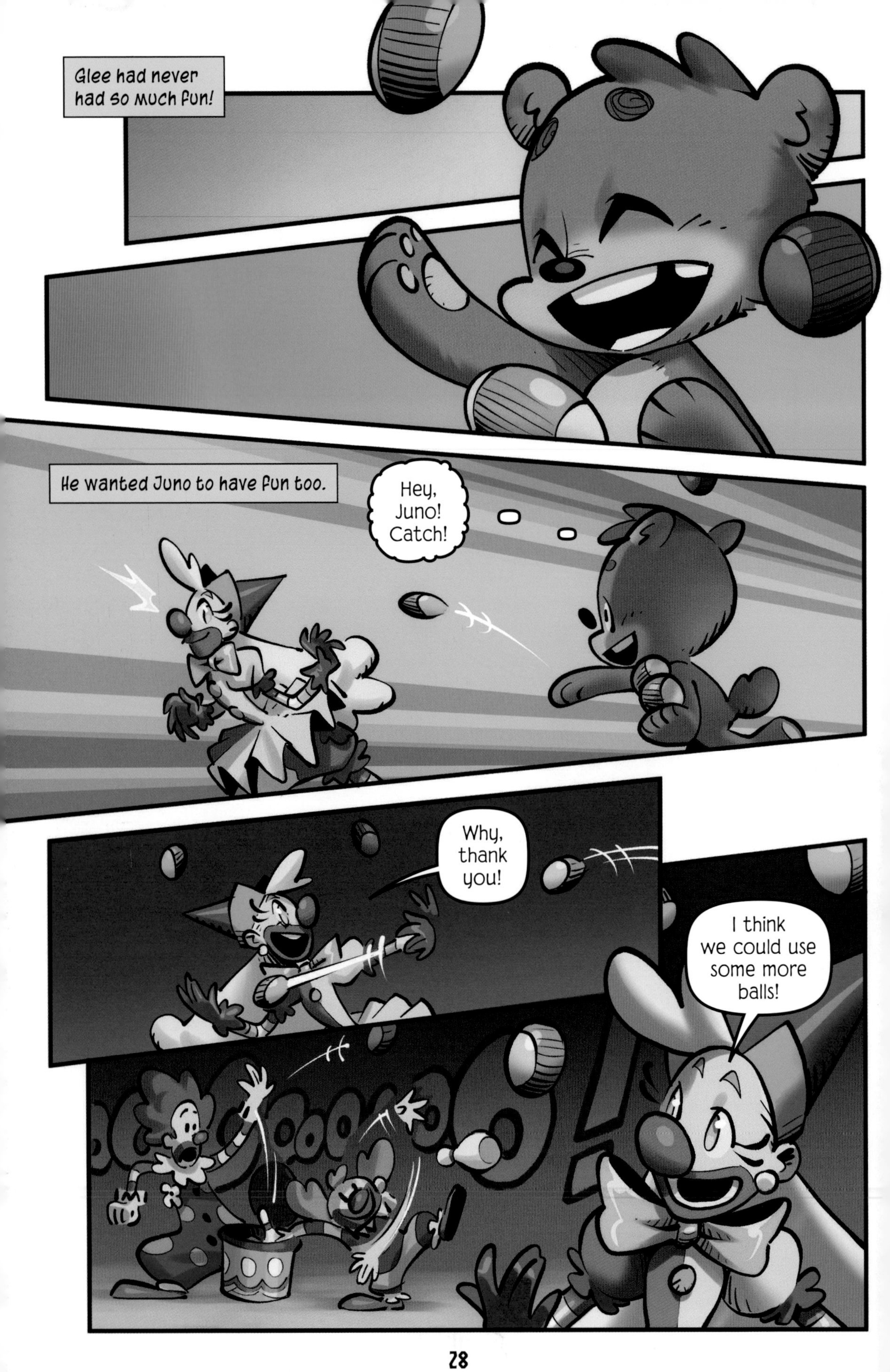

Glee had never had so much fun!
He wanted Juno to have fun too.
Hey, Juno! Catch!
Why, thank you!
I think we could use some more balls!

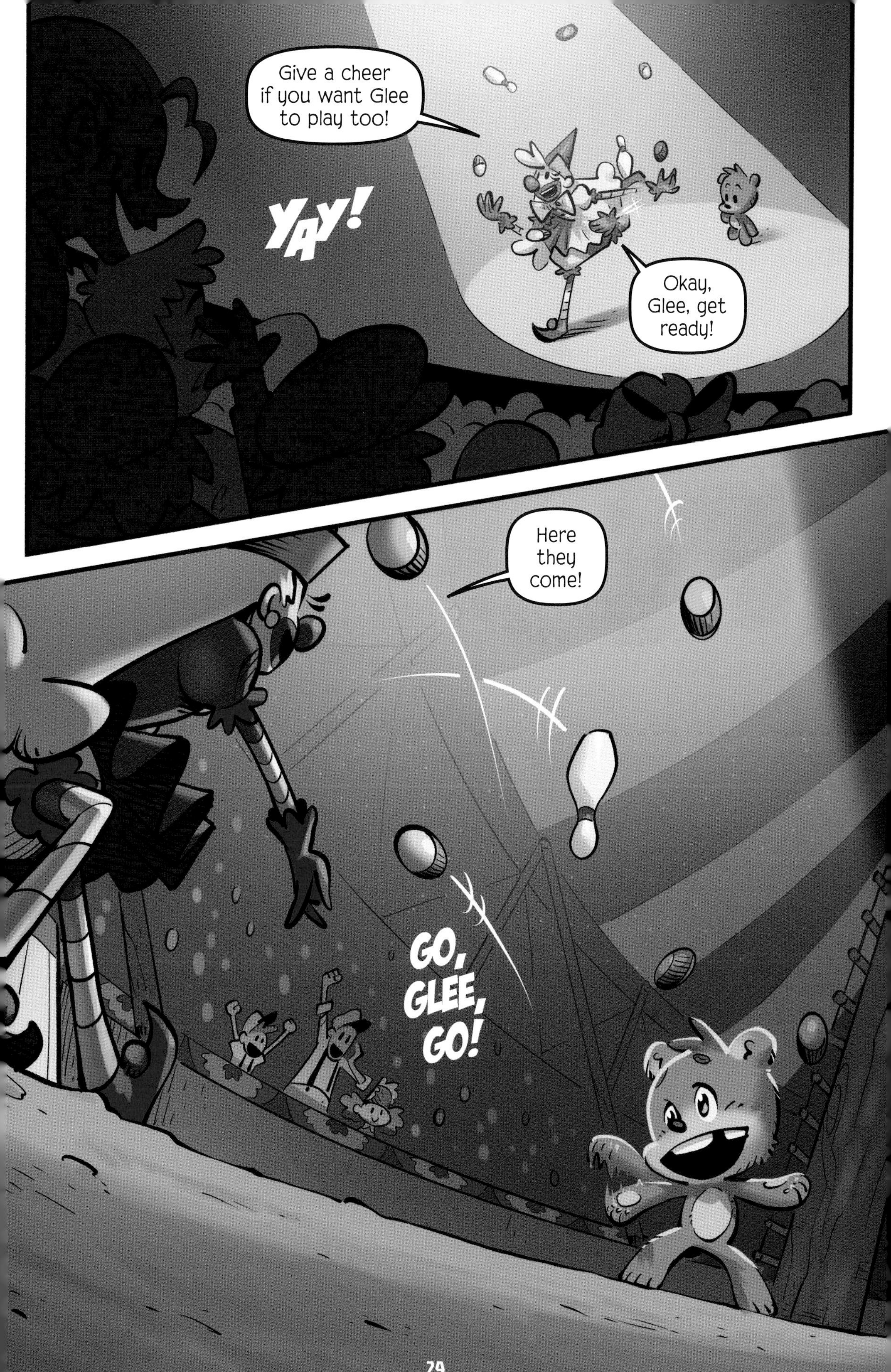

Give a cheer if you want Glee to play too!
YAY!
Okay, Glee, get ready!
Here they come!
GO, GLEE, GO!

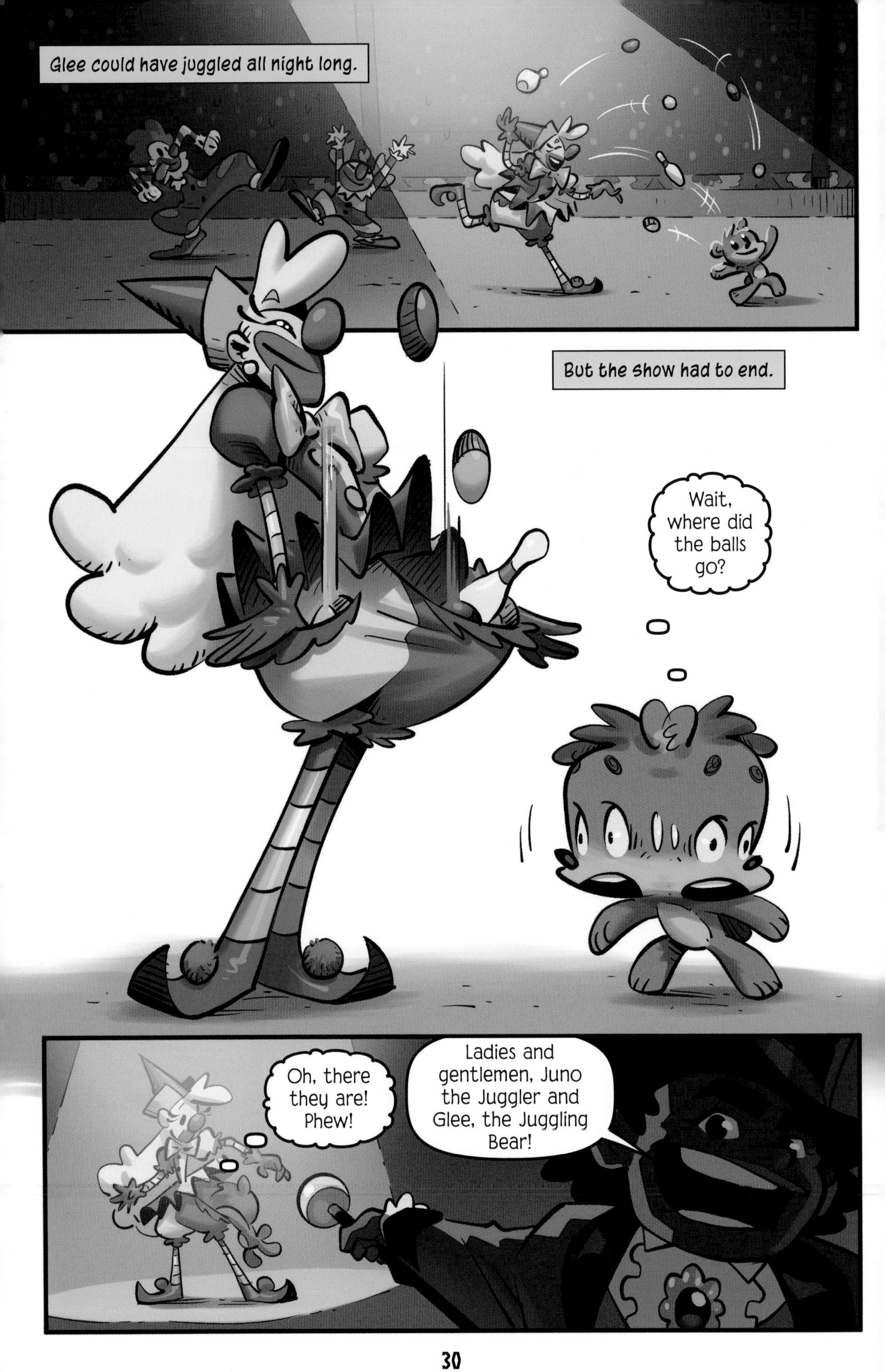
Glee could have juggled all night long.
But the show had to end.
Wait, where did the balls go?
Oh, there they are! Phew!
Ladies and gentlemen, Juno the Juggler and Glee, the Juggling Bear!

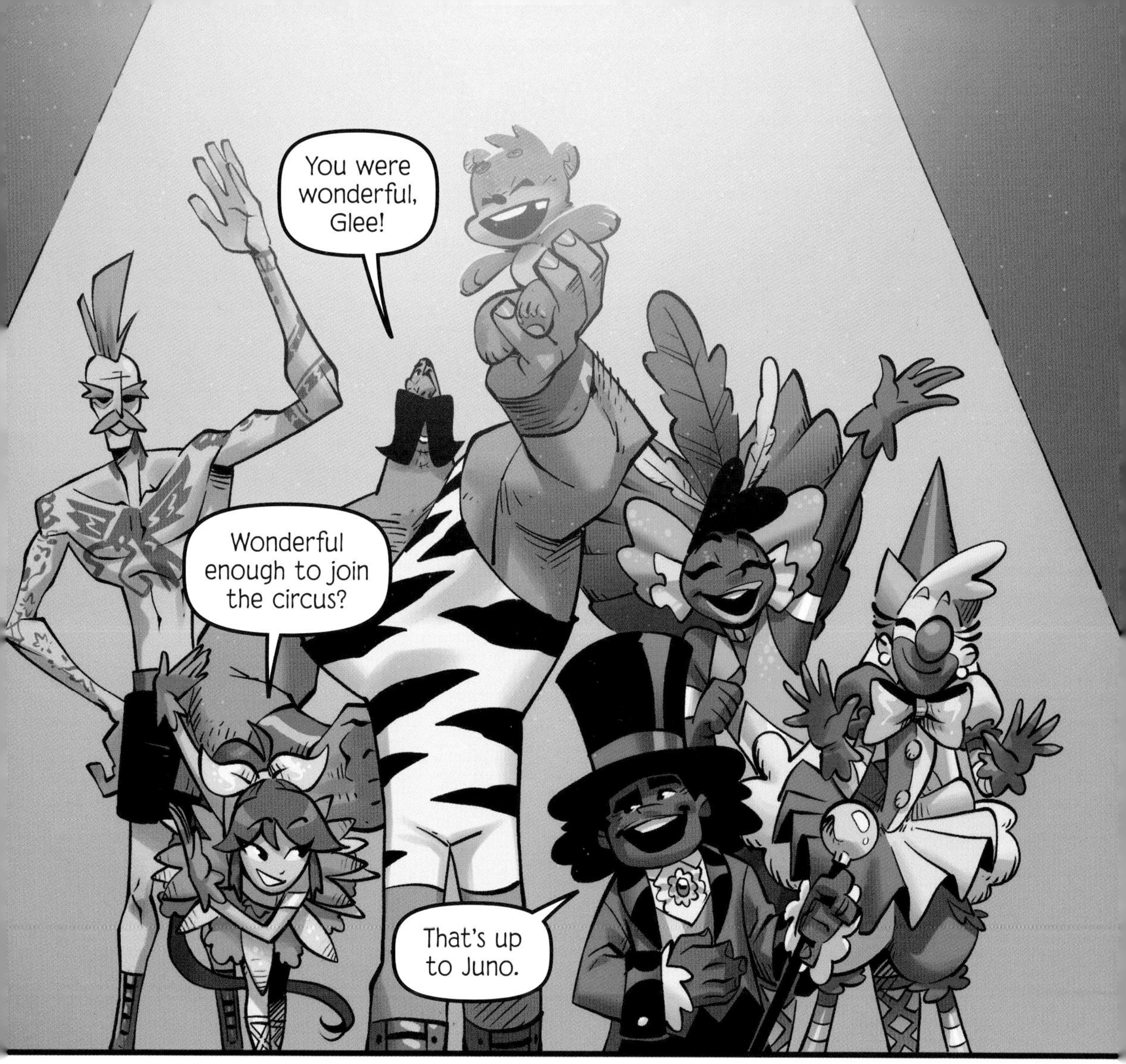
You were wonderful, Glee!
Wonderful enough to join the circus?
That's up to Juno.

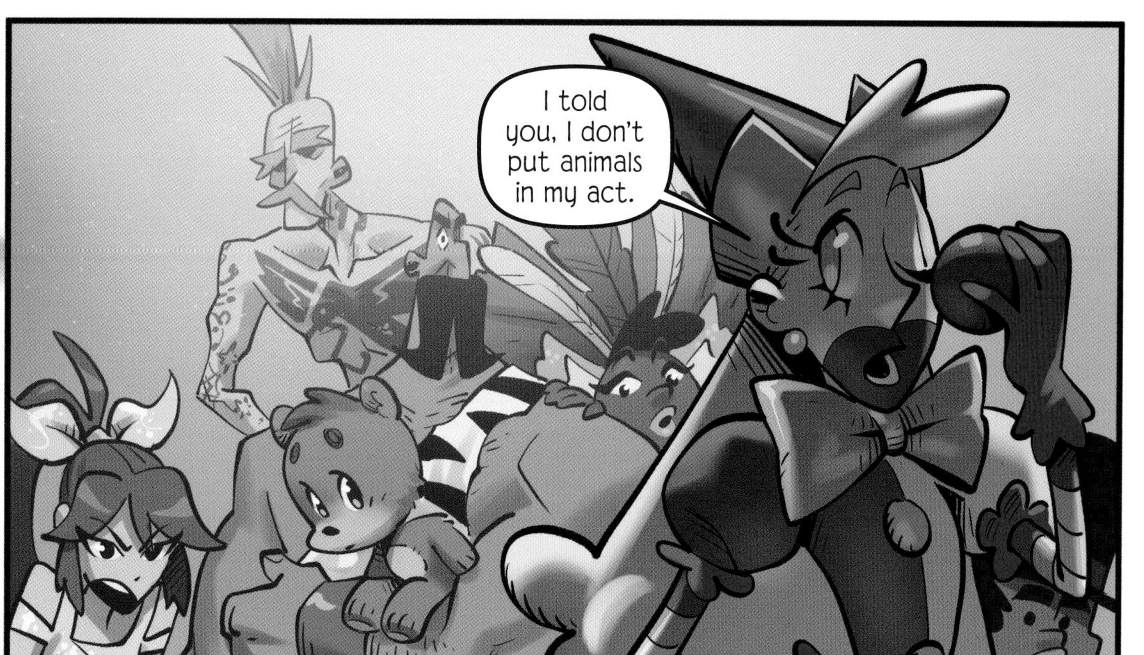
I told you, I don't put animals in my act.

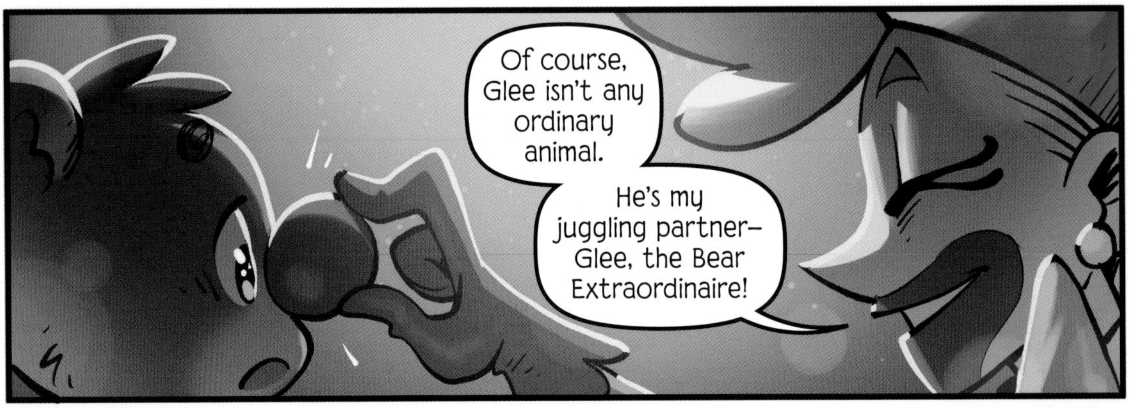
Of course, Glee isn't any ordinary animal.
He's my juggling partner– Glee, the Bear Extraordinaire!

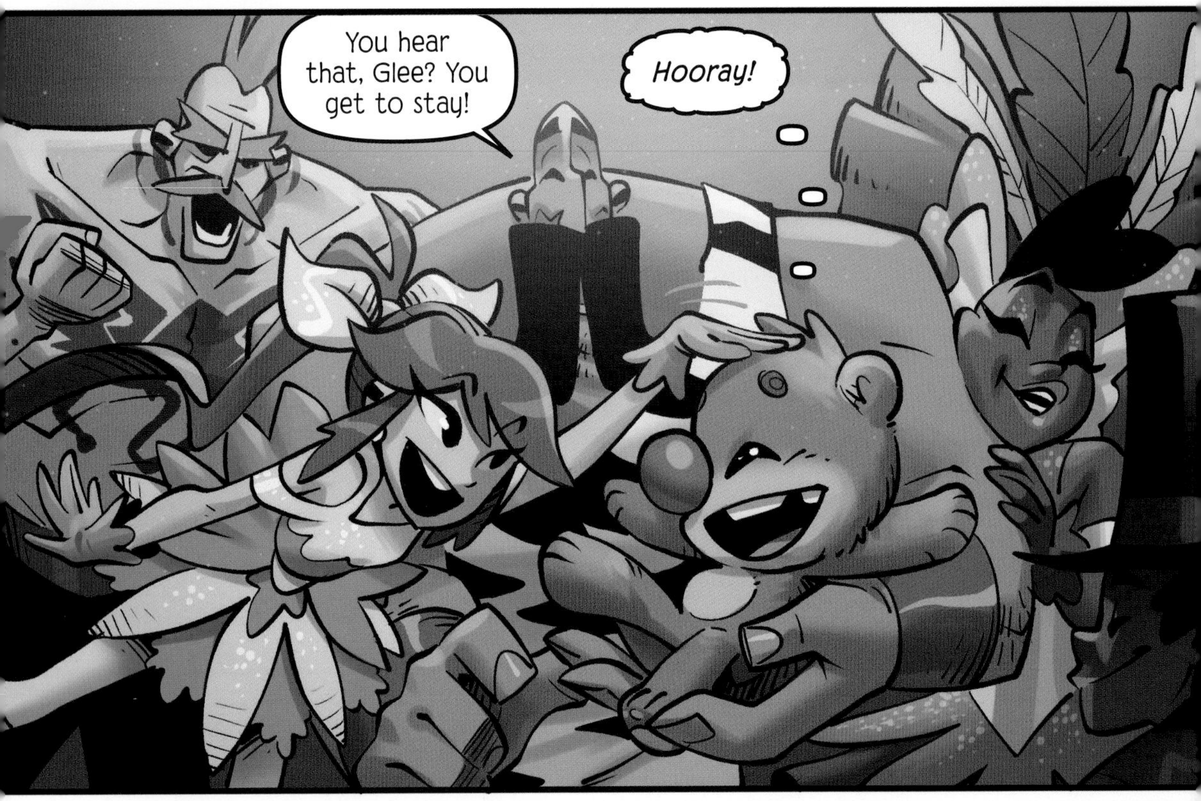
You hear that, Glee? You get to stay!
Hooray!

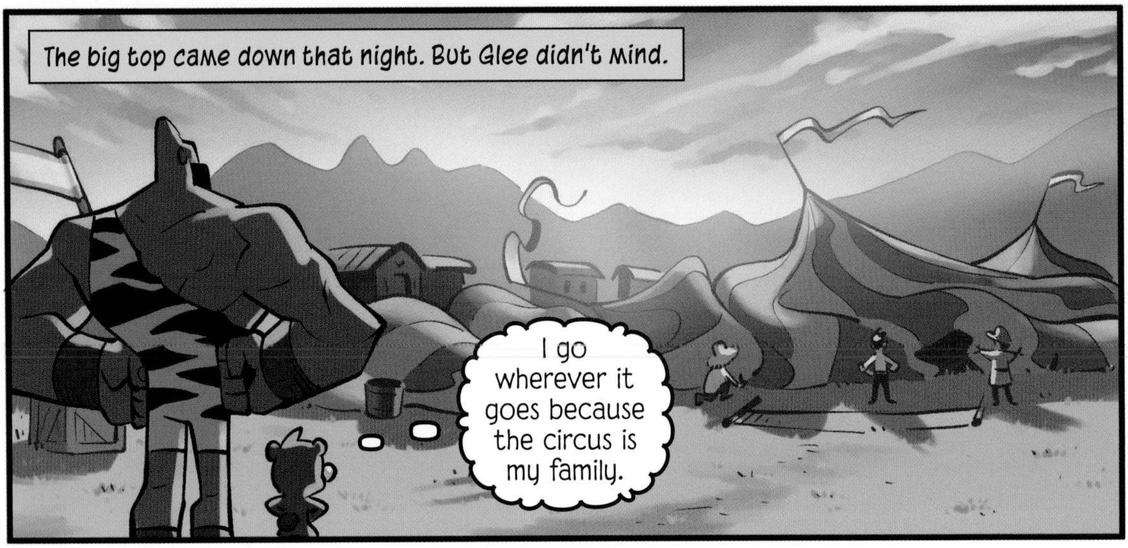
The big top came down that night. But Glee didn't mind.
I go wherever it goes because the circus is my family.

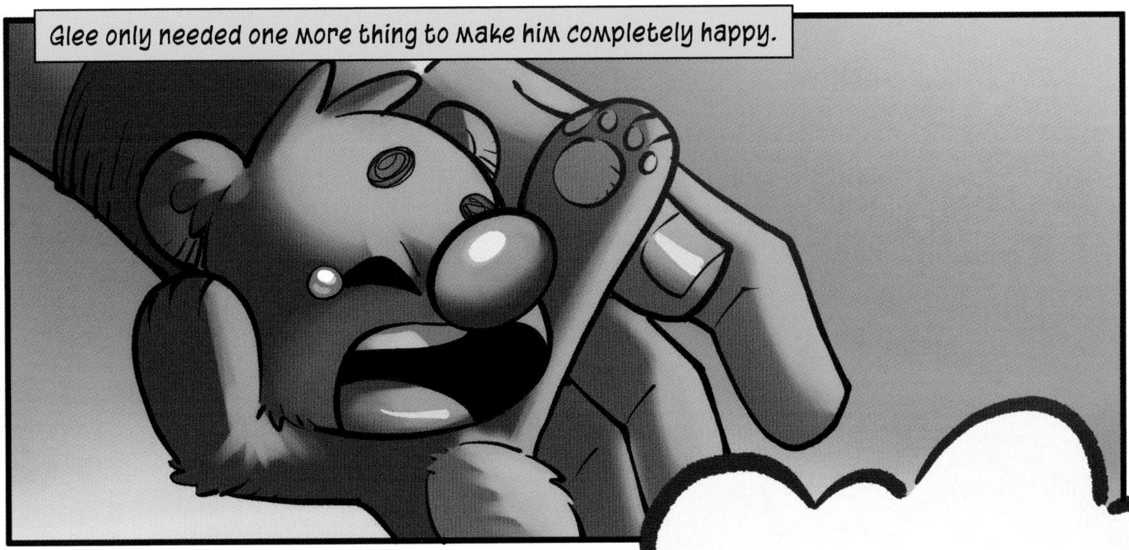
Glee only needed one more thing to make him completely happy.

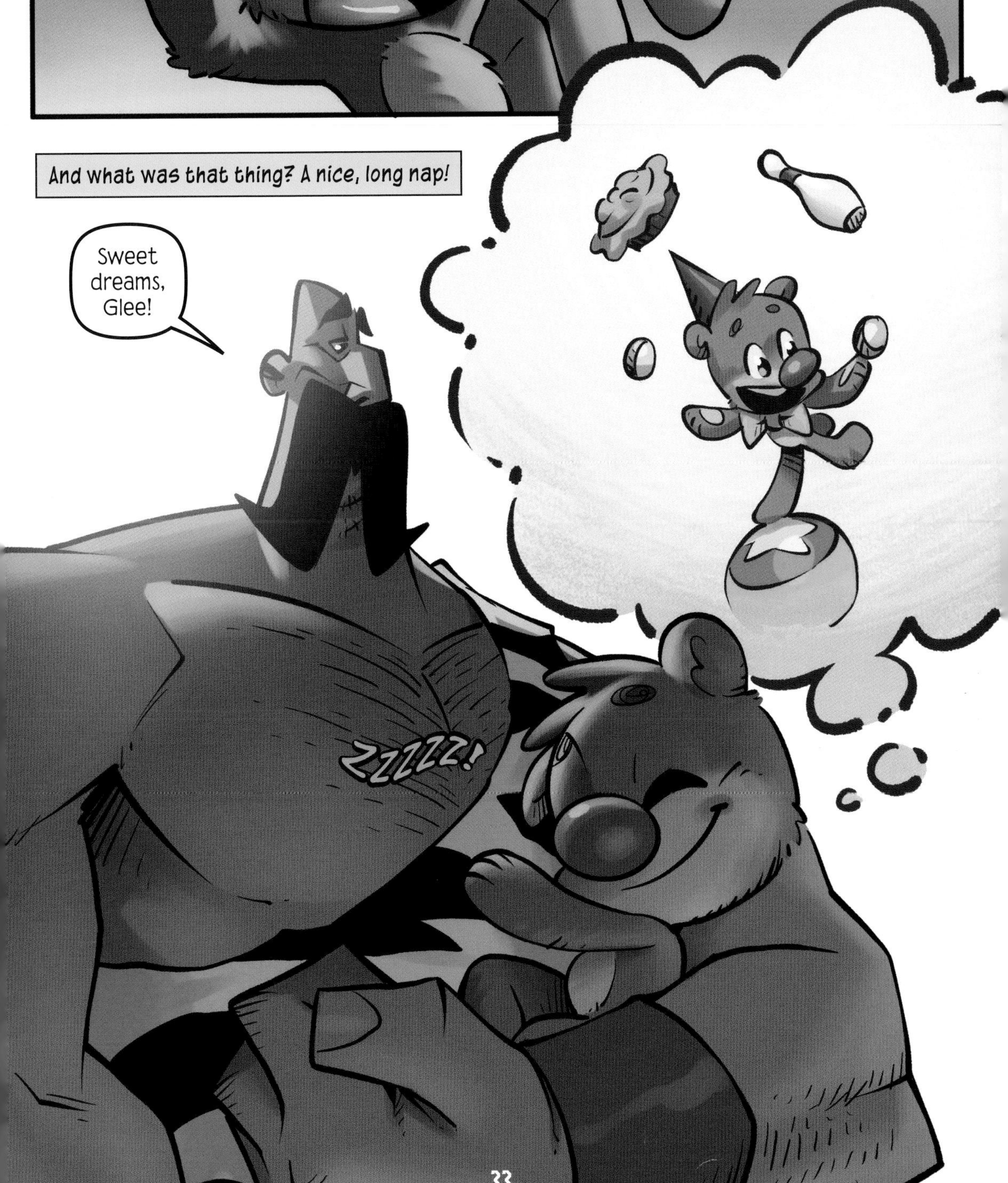
And what was that thing? A nice, long nap!
Sweet dreams, Glee!
ZZZZZ!

ALL ABOUT THE ORIGINAL STORY!

The Juggle Book is based on *The Jungle Book*, a collection of seven short stories by author Rudyard Kipling. The stories are set in a forest in India long ago. The main character is Mowgli, a young orphan boy who is raised by jungle animals. Mowgli's closest friends are Baloo the bear and Bagheera the black panther. They teach Mowgli how to survive in the jungle and overcome his enemies. One story tells how Mowgli defeats Shere Khan, a mean tiger who hates humans, with fire. In another, he escapes Shere Khan's claws thanks to a stampeding herd of buffalo. And after Baloo and Bagheera rescue Mowgli from a band of monkeys, he frees them from a spell cast by a python named Kaa.

Other stories from *The Jungle Book* are just as memorable. There's the tale of Rikki-Tikki-Tavi, a brave mongoose who saves his human family from two deadly cobra attacks. Kotick, a seal with unusual white fur, helps his pod escape from human hunters. And a young boy named Toomai is rewarded for his kindness to elephants. He is allowed to see them dance—something no human had ever seen before.

As endearing as these characters were, none was as beloved as Mowgli. In fact, Kipling wrote five more stories about him in *The Second Jungle Book*. Like all of Kipling's tales about the young boy raised by animals, they are packed with exciting adventures and share valuable lessons about discovering your place in the world.

A FAR OUT GUIDE TO
THE STORY'S SHOW-STOPPING TWISTS

The orphan boy in the original tale is named Mowgli. In this version, the main character is a lonely little bear cub named Glee.

The Jungle Book takes place long ago in a forest in India. *The Juggle Book* is set in a traveling circus.

Mowgli's best friends are a bear and a panther. Glee's best friends are the strongman and a tightrope walker.

A mean tiger wants Mowgli to leave the jungle forever. A juggler named Juno doesn't want Glee to be in her act (but she changes her mind).

VISUAL QUESTIONS

Glee struggles to find a safe place to hibernate in the beginning. Finally, he thinks he has found a good place to sleep. Can you see any clues that his newfound den is actually a train car?

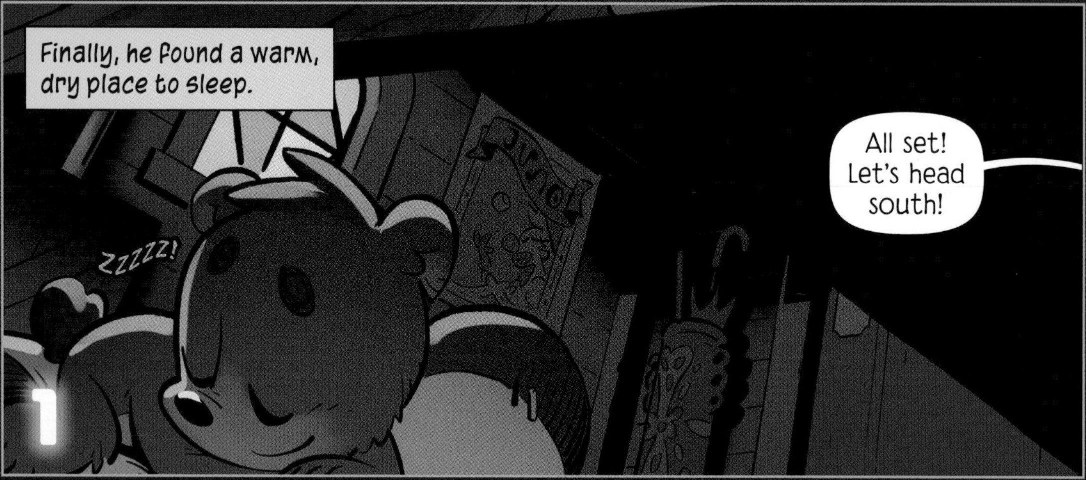
1
Finally, he found a warm, dry place to sleep.
ZZZZZ!
All set! Let's head south!

Illustrations can give hints about what might happen next in a story. Given the way this panel is drawn, what act do you think the performers will have Glee try next?

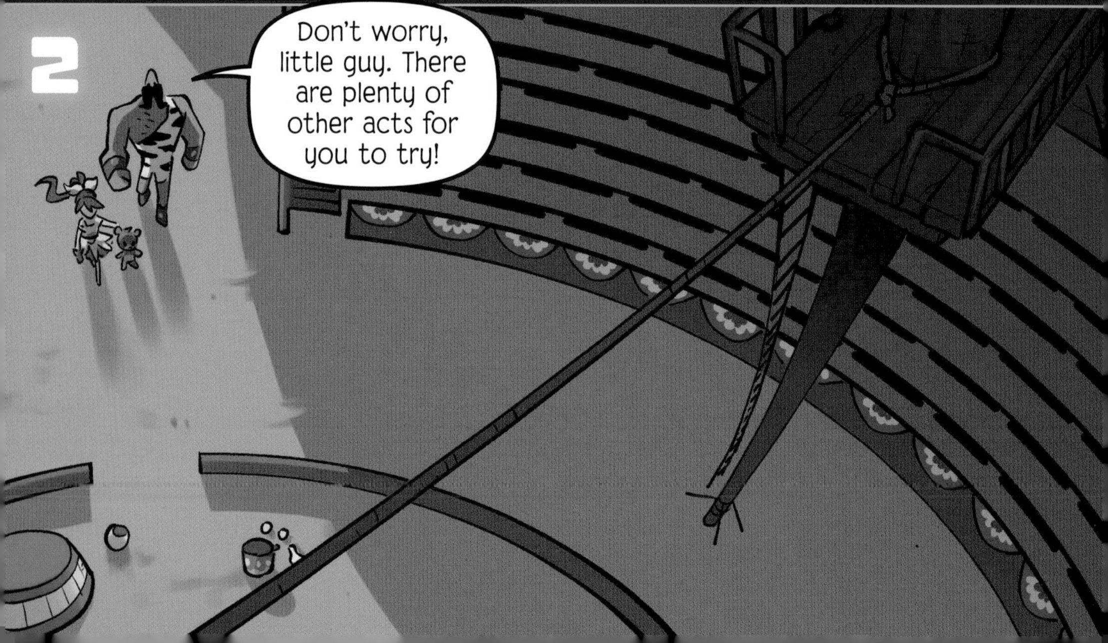
2
Don't worry, little guy. There are plenty of other acts for you to try!

Illustrations can give readers clues about how a character is feeling. Glee can't speak, but how might the strongman be able to tell that Glee does NOT want to try being shot out of a cannon?

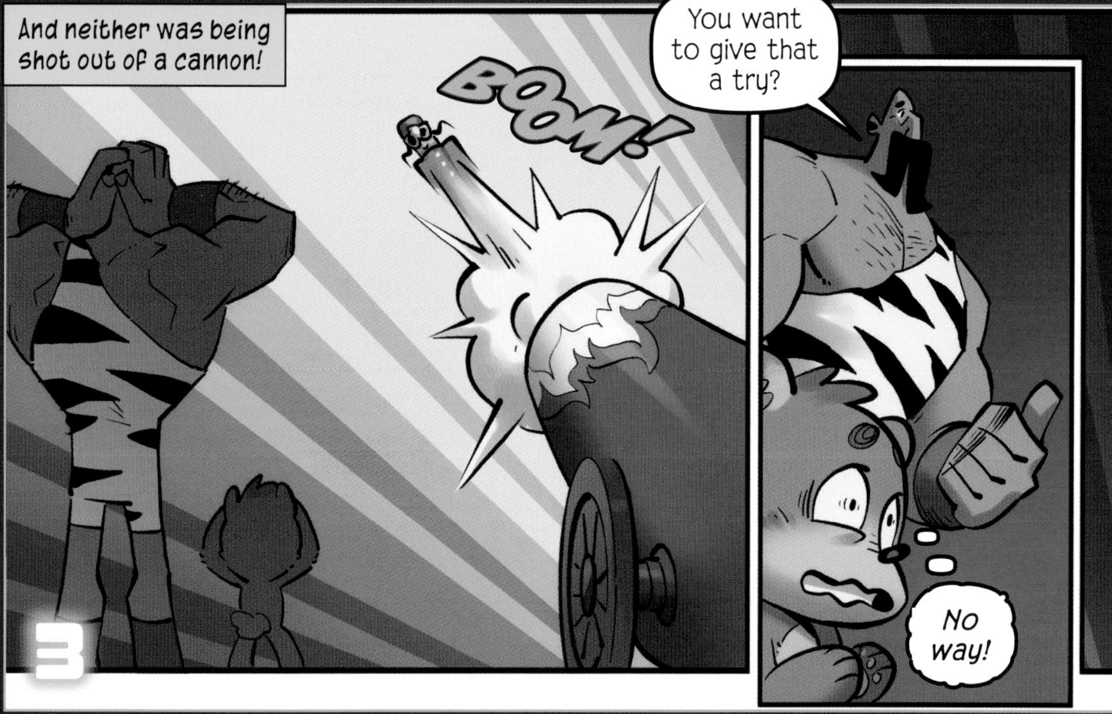
And neither was being shot out of a cannon!
BOOM!
You want to give that a try?
No way!
3

Eventually, Juno agrees to include Glee in her juggling act. What events led up to her changing her mind? What visual cues in the story let you know she is changing her mind?

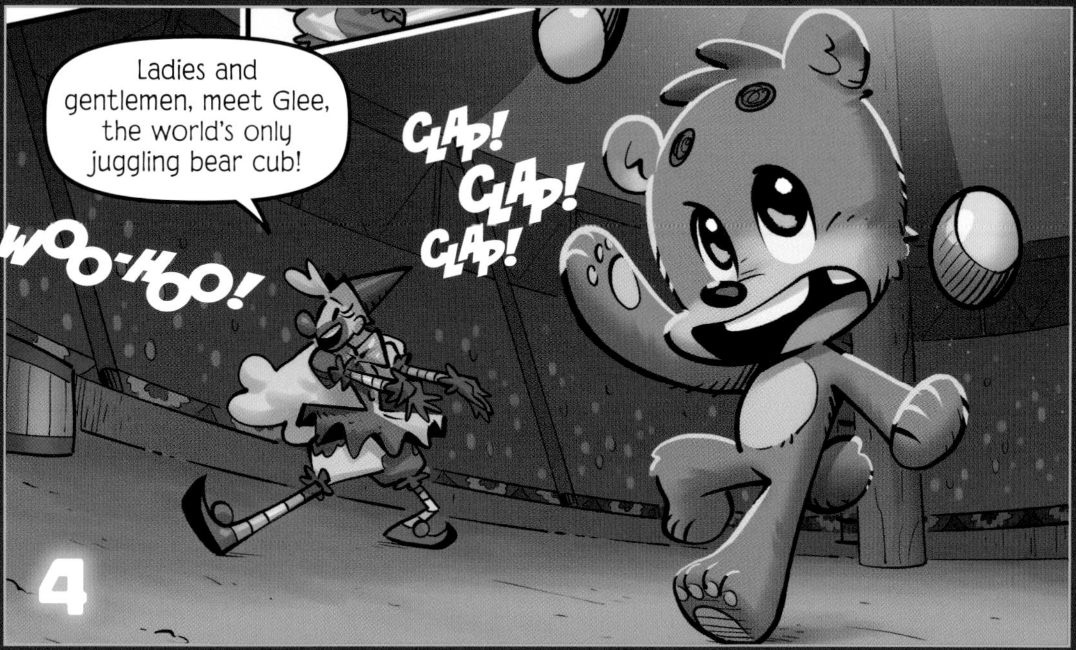
Ladies and gentlemen, meet Glee, the world's only juggling bear cub!
CLAP!
CLAP!
CLAP!
WOO-HOO!
4

AUTHOR

Stephanie True Peters has been writing books for young readers for more than 25 years. Among her most recent titles are *Sleeping Beauty: Magic Master* and *Johnny Slimeseed*, both for Capstone's Far Out Fairy Tales/Folk Tale series. An avid reader, workout enthusiast, and beach wanderer, Stephanie enjoys spending time with her children, Jackson and Chloe, her husband, Dan, and the family's two cats and two rabbits. She lives and works in Mansfield, Massachusetts.

ILLUSTRATOR

Omar Lozano lives in Monterrey, Mexico. He has always been crazy for illustration and is constantly on the lookout for awesome things to draw. In his free time, he watches lots of movies, reads fantasy and sci-fi books, and draws! Omar has worked for Marvel Comics, DC Comics, IDW, Dark Horse Comics, Capstone, and several other publishing companies.

GLOSSARY

cannon (KAN-uhn)–a large, heavy gun that usually has wheels and fires explosives, but in a circus it can fire people

den (DEN)–a place where a wild animal may live; a den may be a hole in the ground or a trunk of a tree or a dark circus boxcar

extraordinaire (ek-STROHR-duh-nare)–something remarkable, like a juggling bear

hibernate (HYE-bur-nate)–to spend winter in a deep sleep

OLD FAVORITES. NEW SPINS.

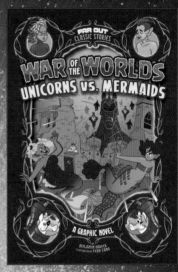

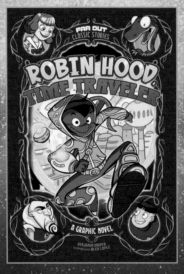

FAR OUT CLASSIC STORIES

ONLY FROM CAPSTONE!